Enduring Love

by

Wanda Dailey

Enduring Love
Copyright 2006
by
Wanda Dailey
Cover design by Renny James

ISBN 1-932196-95-1

Special Delivery Books
WordWright Business Park
46561 State Highway 118
Alpine, TX 79830
Printed in the United States of America

Dedicated to God, who makes all things possible.

To my husband, who is my "Paul,"

to my mother, who said, "I would write my life away,"

and

to my children, whom I love and cherish with all my heart.

Prolog

After seventeen years of marriage to Patrick, finding him in the arms of another woman really hit hard. By comparison, the divorce came in as a close second.

Madison Robertson had no idea what to do with her life. She only hoped it didn't get worse.

She had no words to express the pain of Patrick's betrayal, but she felt as if her world had turned completely upside down. She had no idea when it all began. Looking back, she recognized no warning signs. She only knew that now she and her children had to begin a new life.

Ever since the betrayal, Madie had struggled with all her insecurities, and depended upon her best friend, Gia, to allow her to pour out her heart.

"Gee, Madie, this is really tough," Gia said when Madie told her the news. "We've been through a lot together since elementary school but nothing like this."

Madie wiped the tears from her face.

Gia snapped her fingers. "I know. Let's take a trip to the Bahamas."

"Are you nuts?" Madie sobbed. "I'm in the middle of a divorce. And what do I do with the kids?"

"Not right now, silly. When the divorce is final, let the

kids stay with their Dad for a while. You know, crimp his style, and you and I can take a ship, a plane, heck, we'll swim if we have to. But the Bahamas will do you good."

The final decree came on the coldest January day Boston had ever seen, and the thought of some Bahama sunshine warmed Madie's soul.

Chapter 1

Neither Madie nor Gia slept a wink of their three-hour flight to the islands, and when they stepped from the plane onto the tarmac, the warm, muggy air surrounded them like a blanket.

Madie took a deep breath and closed her eyes at the perfume of the flowers.

"Right this way, ladies." The flight attendant directed them toward customs.

"Would you look at this line?" Gia grumbled. "We're from the States. What do they think we have with us?"

"Relax, Gia. It's moving pretty quickly. Look, it's almost our turn."

"Well, they'd better not mess up my clothes."

"Good afternoon. Passport please."

Gia handed over the little book.

"Thank you, Madam. Would you open your bag for me?"

"Sure, but you'd better not mess up my clothes."

Madie elbowed her friend in the ribs and whispered in her ear. "Quiet, before you really get on this guy's nerves and we have to spend the night in jail.

Luckily, Gia managed to remain civil to the customs

officers and they passed through without incident. They found the car the hotel had sent to pick them up.

"Look, over there," Gia said as she spotted a tall native holding a sign with their names on it.

"I think you're here to pick us up," Gia said.

"Gia and Madie?" he asked while reading the sign.

"That's us," Gia said.

"Please allow me to introduce myself. My name is Carl."

"Nice to meet you, Carl." Madie handed him her luggage. "Is it far to the hotel?"

"No, ma'am, and I think you'll enjoy the ride."

He escorted the travelers to the car and loaded their luggage into the trunk.

Madie and Gia loved the ride to the hotel. They drank in the sight of the flowers and palm trees that lined the streets. Excitement danced in Gia's eyes. Adding to their entertainment, Carl amused his passengers with stories of his family and told about growing up on the island.

"And remember, if you need any help with arrangements of tours or guides just let me know." He handed a business card into the back seat. "Believe me. I know all the beautiful sites on the island."

When they arrived at the hotel, Carl unloaded their luggage and escorted the ladies to the front desk.

As Madie tipped him she said, "Carl, rest assured that if we need a guide, we will definitely contact you."

"Will ya get a load of this place?" Gia twirled herself around 180 degrees. "It's huge."

"I know. I still can't believe I'm here," Madie said.

Once they settled into their room, Madie and Gia

quickly found the balcony that overlooked the beach.

"I think I've died and gone to heaven. It's just so peaceful here," Madie said taking a deep breath of ocean air.

"   And that water goes on for miles," Gia added.

Madie returned to her bags and started to unpack.

"Oh, cut that out, Madie. We're here for a vacation, so let's vacation. Let's go."

"Don't you think we need to freshen up and unpack before we explore? After all, you've got to get out all those great new clothes you bought for the trip."

"You're right. Okay. Let's unpack and then hit the casinos."

Chapter 2

At the first floor casino, Gia led the way to the first blackjack table she could find. Although Gia seemed to understand the game, she didn't have much luck with it. Bored with watching, Madie decided to try her luck at the slot machines. After feeding the machines eighteen of her twenty dollars worth of quarters, Madie felt a tap on her shoulder. She turned to find Gia standing beside her.

"Hey, let's go dancing," Gia suggested.

"I guess. How'd you do at blackjack?"

Gia shrugged her shoulders. "Didn't win anything but I had fun. How about you and slots?"

Madie jiggled her cup. "Only two of the twenty dollars left. Guess I didn't do too well. So where do we go dancing in the Bahamas?"

Gia rolled her eyes. "Like this is a vacation place. There must be gajillions of places to go dancing."

She looked around the casino and spotted something toward the back. "Look, a small dance club right over there. Come on. Wanna go?"

The thought of going dancing without a partner didn't thrill Madie, but she agreed.

They found few people in the club when they arrived,

so easily found a seat. They ordered a drink and listened to the jazz quartet. .

Madie took a long drink from her white wine. "This is incredible. For the first time in years I feel relaxed."

"I know what you mean, but there's not much happening around here," Gia said looking around.

"Perhaps, Miss, I can change all that."

Gia turned to see the handsome man standing behind her.

"Would you care to dance?" he asked.

"Sounds good to me." She leaned over and whispered to Madie, "Watch my stuff," and followed the man onto the dance floor.

As Madie watched them dance, a new customer walked into the club. Madie thought him the most beautiful man she had ever seen. She followed his movements through the club, to the bar, and then to the table where he finally sat down.

His lithe, six-foot figure moved with graceful force, and Madie could feel his presence from across the room. Unbelievable feelings surged through her body. Her heart skipped a beat each time she looked at him. He took her breath away. She didn't ordinarily like long hair on men but his salt and pepper shoulder length ponytail added to his sex appeal.

Madie watched as he walked up to a blonde and asked her to dance. She hoped he hadn't noticed her staring, but felt that he had.

Stop it, Madie. Stop staring. But she couldn't help being drawn to him. She watched him dance at least three more times and noticed he could dance very well. He moved to every beat of the song.

She felt flushed with the realization that she wanted to meet him. She should go up to him and introduce herself, but couldn't muster the courage. Gia was still dancing with her handsome partner and waved good-bye. Madie would go back to the room.

Back in the room, Madie changed her clothes and poured herself a glass of wine. She stepped out onto the balcony to enjoy the moonlight splayed across the waves and breathe in the fresh ocean air. But her thoughts continued to drift to the nameless man who had taken over her thoughts, and she felt very strange and confused.

"What's wrong with me?" she muttered to herself. "I'm a levelheaded woman. I don't believe in love at first sight, but here I am in the Bahamas, thinking about a man that I've seen exactly once."

She shook her head and took another sip of wine. "I'll probably never see him again, but I hope I do."

The wine warmed her and she shed the light robe she had donned. "Okay, so I'm a thirty-something mother of three, but I'm not bad looking. Some people have even called me beautiful. Why couldn't I attract that guy, or somebody like him?"

Madie swallowed the last of her wine and headed for bed. A few minutes later, the wine had arrived and she drifted off to a deep sleep. She never even heard Gia return to the room.

"Wake up sleepy head."

Gia's voice intruded on her dreams.

"Come on. Do you intend to sleep our vacation away?"

Madie moaned and rolled over to face her roommate.

"Oh, you're back."

"Sure I'm back. Got in about one this morning. Had a great time dancing. But he really wasn't my type. Let's get up, get some breakfast and go shopping. Someone told me the Straw Market's a great place to go for souvenirs."

At the end of the day, Madie and Gia found themselves back in their hotel room.

"So what do you want to do tonight?" Madie asked.

"Well, ah, last night, I met a very nice man and he asked me to have dinner with him tonight. Is that all right with you?"

"Sure, you don't have to get my permission. You're a big girl. Besides, I'm happy for you. I'll probably take in one of the shows. You don't need to worry about me. I'm a big girl, too. So, how late do you think you'll be?"

Gia shrugged her shoulders. "Don't know. I don't know what he has in mind."

"Well, how about if I meet you in the dance club around midnight?"

As planned, Madie went to the show but was disappointed. It turned out to be far less spectacular than presented. After the show, she made her way to the dance club to meet Gia. She ordered a drink and as she sipped on her white wine, the man she had seen the night before walked in.

She thought she felt her heart skip a beat, and just when she had thought she had put him completely out of her mind. He looked right past her, and never gave her a second glance.

Her heart pounded. He was as beautiful as she remembered and she wanted to meet him. She forced herself calm down, and even out her breathing. Then she tried to figure out what there was about this man that drew her to him.

He stood at the end of the bar and Madie told herself, it's now or never. She gathered up her courage and slowly made my way toward him. Little by little, she sidled toward him until she stood next to him. He stood with his back to her and she tried to figure out how to strike up a conversation with him.

The next thing she knew, she lost her balance and accidentally bumped into him. She felt herself blush when he turned. "Oh, I'm so sorry. I didn't mean to, oh dear." Madie grabbed a nearby napkin and found herself wiping dribbles of white wine from his jacket sleeve.

"Quite all right. No problem. Please don't give it another thought. Actually, I would hope you'd excuse me. I must have moved into you."

She stared at him open-mouthed as British accent wrapped itself around her like a warm blanket.

He then turned back around and didn't give her another glance.

Bereft and embarrassed, Madie had no idea what to do next. She had never been very good at flirting. Then she thought that maybe the direct approach would work best.

She tapped him on the shoulder. He turned, and she swallowed hard.

"I'm sorry to bother you again. But do you know of any good dance clubs on the island?"

There it was. That British accent again, and Madie melted when he said,

"Oh, Miss, I know of many but wouldn't recommend

any because I don't think any of them would be very safe."

Her heart raced.

He offered his hand. "Paul Nobles here. I've lived most of my life here so I know this place. You're probably in the safest place you could be, right here. Believe me, this island has many bad characters who would take advantage of a tourist."

Still holding his hand, she said, "Thank you for your concern, Paul. My name is Madie."

They spent the next few minutes talking about the island, the weather, and the great hotel food. Finally, Paul asked, "Would you like to dance?"

As his arms wrapped around her, she couldn't believe that she was dancing in his arms. She reveled in the sensation.

"My but we dance well for two people who have just met," Paul commented.

Madie agreed and rested her head on his shoulder. All the while she wondered how she had come into this good luck.

Madie and Paul danced through several songs, when Paul suggested, "How about if we find a table and order a drink?"

Madie agreed and she followed Paul as he led her to a nearby table.

"So whatta ya have?" The waitress seemed to have come out of nowhere. She smacked the gum in her mouth until it popped.

"A double martini for me, and the lady will have...? He looked to Madie.

"A white wine please."

"Sure. Be right back." She blew a bubble that filled her face before she turned toward the bar.

A few minutes later, the waitress placed the drinks on the table and Paul pulled a few bills from his wallet and handed them to her.

"Thanks." She blew another bubble and graced him with a wink.

Just then, Gia bounded toward them.

"Madie! There you are," she said breathlessly.

Paul rose at her arrival.

"Oh, don't get up for me. I'm Gia."

"Nice to meet you, Gia. I'm Paul." He looked at Madie.

"This is the traveling companion I told you about," Madie said.

"Then indeed, very nice to meet you."

Gia looked wide-eyed at Madie. "Where'd you find this hunk?"

"Gia!"

"Actually, Gia, I found Madie, and I feel fortunate to have done so."

"Well, la-de-da, British to boot! Don't you love the accent? Anyway, I just came to tell you I won't be getting back to our room until late. No need to wait up for me." Then she whirled around and nearly ran from the club.

Paul gave Madie a surprised look. "Is she always so reserved?"

Madie laughed at his choice of words. "Gia's having the time of her life, and she's always tended toward the very excitable end of the emotional spectrum."

"Well, I'm glad she's having fun. Now, let's have

some more fun. Would you like a walk on the beach?"

"But our drinks."

"We'll take them with us."

Madie felt she probably shouldn't, but couldn't find the strength to say no.

The full moon lit the beach and the water. They saw every wave that crashed onto the sand, and every sand crab that scurried from hole to hole. They walked several hundred yards down the beach, at the edge of the surf until Paul asked if she'd like to sit.

When they had found a boulder, Madie made herself comfortable and Paul sat beside her.

"You know, this is rather unlike me. I'm not in the habit of walking on the beach with new acquaintances."

Madie smiled and hoped it was true.

"You know, I saw you at the club dancing last night. You're really a very good dancer."

He smiled.

Madie felt so happy to be sitting here with him, but couldn't explain the feelings that flowed through her.

Suddenly he pulled her close. Though no innocent virgin, she hesitated.

"Are you married, Madie?"

She told him about her ex-husband and his new love.

He said, "I don't understand how any man would be so stupid to do that to someone as beautiful as you."

Madie blushed. "Thank you, Paul. Do you know how good you are for my ego?"

"Madie, a mean it. Truly."

He sounded sincere.

Then, without warning, he leaned closer and kissed

her. Madie felt her knees go weak.

Breathlessly, Paul broke off the kiss and cleared his throat. "Madie, maybe we'd better go back to the hotel."

Back at the hotel, they shared a chaste kiss.

"Gia won't be back for hours yet. Would you like to come up to my room?"

"I wish I could, but I can't tonight, Madie."

She wondered what he'd have planned for so late, but put the thought out of her mind.

"What's your room number? I'd like to take you to dinner tomorrow night. That is, if you're available."

"I'm available and yes, I'd love to have dinner with you."

When she gave him her room number, he kissed her cheek. "Good night, Madie."

Back in her room her mind kept busy with thoughts of Paul, so different from any man she had ever met. He occupied every thought that crossed her mind that night, and she eagerly waited to see him again on the next day.

Gia bounced into the room less than an hour later. With a squeal she asked, "So who was that gorgeous man you were with?"

"I met him at the dance club and I'm seeing him again tomorrow night."

Madie and Gia talked for the next hour talking about the men they had met, like two schoolgirls sharing secrets.

Chapter 3

The next morning, Madie woke up thinking about Paul and her feelings for him. None of it made any sense. She barely knew him. Maybe she and Paul were just meant to be.

Gia finally woke up around noon and they went to the beach where they enjoyed the white sand and turquoise water. Palm trees blew in the breeze and the tropical sun warmed their skin.

Late in the afternoon, Madie noted the time. "Gia, it's already 5:00. I think I'll go back to the room and get ready for dinner with Paul."

"Fine. I'll see you in a little while. I just want to soak up some more sun."

Fifteen minutes after Madie arrived in her room, the phone rang. Her heart sank. That had to be one of the kids with a crisis. Paul's voice pleasantly surprised her.

"Madie, I've been thinking about you all day. Could you meet me in the lobby at seven?"

Her stomach suddenly felt full of butterflies. "Paul, how nice of you to say that. Thank you. Yes, I can meet you at seven."

Madie's anxiety level soared. What was she getting into?

Madie changed five times before she decided on a floral sundress. When Gia returned, she asked, "Does this look okay?"

"Why so nervous? You look fine. It's just a dinner date."

"You know, you're right." But she dared not share her true thoughts and feelings with Gia.

Shortly before seven, Madie took up her purse and wrap and headed for the door. "See you later, Gia. Have a good time."

"Have a good time yourself!"

When Madie arrived downstairs, she sat where she knew Paul could see her. By 8:30, he had still not arrived. Irritated, she went to the nearest bar and ordered a drink. By the time she sipped on her second white wine, she felt as though someone stared at her.

She turned to see Paul standing behind her. He leaned toward her, kissed her cheek, and sat beside her.

"So sorry, luv. I'm not usually late. So glad to see you didn't leave. I was home with my son. He's been home sick all day. I stayed with him until he fell asleep."

Madie stood up and made to leave.

He grabbed her arm. "Madie please don't leave. I am telling you the truth."

Something inside her allowed for his honesty, so she sat back down.

"Thank you for staying, Madie. Let me buy you a drink."

Over drinks, he told her about his children and how much he loved them. He told her of Paul Jr. who married and doing well in his own business. Then, there was Adrian, at college in Florida and he spoke of his only daughter with pride, Sarah.

"Oh, Sarah's so beautiful but very headstrong." His eyes lit up when he spoke of his youngest child. "Peter's very much like me when I was a child. As a parent, you're not supposed to have any favorites, but I have to confess that Peter is my favorite."

By the way he spoke of his children, he gave Madie the impression of an involved father, and this added to her comfort level with him. She wished her children had had such a good father. Instead, they had a man who rarely called them by name.

She shook away all thought of Patrick and her failed marriage. Tonight, she wanted to enjoy her evening with Paul.

"So where will we go for dinner?" she asked. "I've made reservations at a very exclusive restaurant on the island. I think you'll enjoy it very much."

"I'm starving. Let's go."

Madie let Paul order for her because of his familiarity with the menu. Madie didn't quite know what entrée filled her plate but she found it delicious, and Paul enjoyed watching her eat, which made her feel self-conscience.

They finally left the restaurant at about eleven thirty, and Paul took her back to her hotel.

Once again she asked, "Would you like to come up to my room?"

"Oh, Madie, I'd love to, but I need to get home to check on Peter. I'll call you tomorrow."

"I understand," she whispered.

Once again he kissed her on the cheek and left her

alone.

Madie didn't understand how she could want him so badly. Upstairs in her room, she felt empty and alone. How could this man mean so much to her so soon?

Gia walked in and interrupted her thoughts with a million questions.

"So where did you go for dinner? Was the food good? Is he romantic? What did you do afterward?"

"Geez, Gia. One thing at a time." Madie told her friend about her evening with Paul and that he left early to go home and check on his son.

Gia looked at her and laughed. "Madie, are you so naive that you'd believe some bullshit story like that?"

"Gia, what are you saying? You're my best friend. You're just jealous. That's what this is all about. You just need to shut up or you'll spend the rest of our trip alone."

"All right. All right. So you want to hear about my date with Dave?"

"Sure."

"I'm having so much fun. Dave is such a great guy, and I'm going to see him again tomorrow night."

Still miffed, Madie said, "That's great. I'm glad you're having fun, but I'm ready for bed. I'll see you in the morning."

Madie didn't want to think about Gia's earlier comment, but she wondered. She slept lightly that night and woke up tired.

When Gia woke up they decided to spend their last full day on the island riding jet skis.

When they returned to their room about four that afternoon, they found the phone flashing a message. Madie called the front desk and learned she had a message from Paul.

"Madie, luv, hope you can meet me at the dance club tonight at eight."

She smiled at the message and told Gia of her plans.

"I'm glad he called, Madie. I'm sorry for the things I said last night about Paul."

Madie accepted her apology and the friends hugged.

"Okay, let's shower and get ready for more fun," Gia said.

"Sounds like a plan." Madie headed for the closet to pick out an outfit and Gia headed for the bathroom.

Gia poked her head out of the bathroom door. "By the way, Madie, would it be all right with you if I didn't come back to the room tonight?'

"I'm a big girl, and so are you. Have a great time. Just be careful."

Gia left well before 8:00, leaving Madie to grow nervous again. She felt like a silly teenager. Just before eight, she went downstairs and waited for Paul at the club.

She sat watching a couple on the dance floor. They looked as though they were on their honeymoon, because they looked so much in love. She looked at her watch again, and wished Paul would hurry up because she wanted to see him so badly.

She turned to get the waitress's attention to order a drink and then she saw him. He stood in the doorway dressed in white pants and white shirt and looked like something out of a dream. As he walked toward her, her heart raced so fast, she feared it might stop. She trembled but tried hard to keep her composure. She didn't want him to know the effect he had on her.

When he leaned down to kiss her, she jumped at his touch.

He smiled. "I'm so glad to see you. You look beautiful." He then took her hand and led her to the dance floor.

As they danced to a slow song, Madie allowed herself to believe they had grown close. She didn't want to leave him tomorrow. They didn't speak a word the whole time they danced, because no words were needed. Madie felt as though she could have died that very night in his arms and would have been the happiest woman in the world.

They left the dance floor and sat down at a nearby table to have a drink.

Paul looked into Madie's eyes. "Madie, don't leave tomorrow."

She couldn't believe what she had heard. Paul had expressed exactly what she was feeling.

"Paul, I wish I could stay, but I have children too."

"I understand. You're a mother first. I respect that." He kissed her hand. "But we have tonight. Let's make the most of it."

Gia won't be back to the room tonight. Come up with me."

He smiled and took her hand, then let her lead the way.

In the elevator she wondered if it was possible that Paul shared her feelings. Her stomach felt queasy and she felt as though her knees would give out at any moment, when Paul pulled her to him and kissed her as she had never been kissed before.

She went limp in his arms and when the elevator

opened at her floor, she could barely walk to her room. She opened the door and Paul immediately picked her up and carried her in.

He carried her to the bed and started kissing her neck, her arms, and her face. She felt weak and overwhelmed by his kisses. She couldn't think straight.

Ever so slowly, he started to remove her clothes. His fingers barely brushed her skin, and chills traveled through her body.

"Madie, I've never wanted any woman as much as I want you. I'm afraid of what I'm feeling. All I know is I have to have you."

His words, his body, his touch, all felt wonderful and mirrored everything that she had thought and felt these past three days.

He admired her body and touched her, brushing his fingers up and down her limbs. "You're so warm and soft."

She felt calm in his arms and when he kissed her, she felt as though he were sucking her breath from her body. He took his time in making love to her.

Madie gave in to every calling of his voice, hands and mouth without reservation. She kept looking at him to make sure this was truly happening, never taking her gaze from his eyes. She felt as she had gone to heaven and never wanted to leave.

When he finally decided he had nearly driven her mad, he entered her with such gentleness. Madie felt as if she'd explode with each deep thrust. He drove her senseless and she didn't care. No one had ever made love to her like this before. She never wanted him to stop, and she began to cry.

"Oh, Madie, don't cry. Have I hurt you, luv?"

She sniffed. "No, Paul. You haven't hurt me. Please, just please don't stop."

Together, they exploded in a maelstrom of emotions, and physically spent. They lay in each other's arms unable to move. She began seriously considering not leaving tomorrow, but knew she had to go back home. She also came to think she had fallen in love with Paul and it was like nothing she had ever felt before.

"Please, Madie, is there any way you can stay? Any way you don't have to leave tomorrow?"

She started to cry. "Paul, I don't want to leave you, but I have to go home to my children."

She noticed that he too had begun to cry.

"I promise, I'll see you again one day, soon. Don't forget me, Madie." He gave a little chuckle. "Our love is as dangerous as Bonnie and Clyde, but we'll be together someday, somehow."

She wondered at Paul's use of the word love. Then he held her close and called her his Bonnie. Through his tears he said, "I love you, Madie."

She couldn't believe her ears. She had never known any man to be as sincere as Paul.

"Oh, Paul, I love you too. I dared not hope."

"But I do love you. I can't explain it."

"Neither can I."

He rose from the bed and began to dress, then he walked over to the bed. "I've never had these feelings for anyone before. I can't just let you go home without the hope of ever seeing you again. Please tell me we can meet again, sometime soon."

"Paul, you know I'll do my best. I have to see you

again soon."

The lovers said their tearful good-byes and Madie walked him to the door. She didn't want him to go and held onto him until his jacket sleeve slipped through her fingers. He kissed her one last time.

"I'll see you again soon, my Bonnie. Remember I love you."

Madie watched as he disappeared around the corner, then she collapsed to the floor crying asking God to help her with the pain of loss.

She wasn't sure why she had met Paul, but she knew she loved him and wanted a life with him. She tried not to think about leaving, but it filled her thoughts along with wondering when she would see Paul again.

Chapter 4

The next morning, Madie and Gia packed and went to the airport. They passed through customs without any problems and caught their flight home.

During their flight, Gia kept saying how much she loved the Bahamas and that they should try to come back every year. All Madie could think about was Paul and she wondered if she'd ever see him.

"So did you have a good time with Paul," Gia asked.

"Oh, Gia, I had a wonderful time with him. I so much want to see him again."

"Is he married?"

"You know, I don't know. I never even asked him. The thought never crossed my mind."

"Why didn't you ask?" Gia wondered.

"I guess I really didn't want to know." She tried not to think about the possibility of Paul being married.

When Madie and Gia landed in Boston around five that evening, the weather was still very cold.

"Geesh, we should have stayed in the Bahamas. At least the weather there was warm." Gia shivered and hugged herself to keep out the cold.

"Believe me, I agree." But more than anything, Madie

wished to be back in the Bahamas to be with Paul.

Once home, Madie's children greeted her with all kinds of questions.

"Did you have a good time?"

"Did you go snorkeling?"

"What was it like?"

"What did you bring us?"

Josh, her oldest son asked, "So you think you'd like to go back someday?"

Madie smiled. "Sure would, and I'd like to take you all with me. I know you'd love it there."

Her daughter Margaret studied her mother intently and then asked, "Why do you seem so happy? I haven't seen you like this in a long time."

Madie suppressed the bubble of a giggle. "I'm just so relaxed."

She seemed to accept the reason and the excitement about their mother's return continued. Madie knew she couldn't tell her children about Paul, mainly because she had no idea about where their relationship was going.

Her other son, John, told Madie he loved the T-shirt she had picked out for him and he was glad to see she enjoyed her vacation. Though happy to see her children, Madie felt melancholy about leaving the new love she had found in the Bahamas.

That night, Madie went to bed early. She knew she had to go into the office first thing in the morning. She kissed each of her children goodnight and headed for bed. It felt good being home, but she felt empty inside. She missed Paul.

The next day at the office, everyone wanted a rundown

of her vacation. Gia supplied most of the details while Madie buried herself in her work. Then the phone rang.

"Madie here, can I help you?"

"Hello, Bonnie." Paul's voice caused a jolt of electricity to sizzle through her.

"Oh, Paul, what a nice surprise."

"Just calling to make sure you got home safely."

"Yes, I did. Thank you for asking. How are you?"

"I miss you. Meet me next month in Miami," he pleaded.

"I don't know. What with the kids and all. Let me find out. I'll call you as soon as I can. Why Miami?"

"I just thought it might be easier on you if we met there and then too we could spend more time together in Miami rather than the Bahamas."

"Let me see what I can do. I'd love to meet you there next month."

"I just have to see you, Madie. You're all I think about."

His words made her absolutely ecstatic to know that he could possibly be in love with her too.

"Thank you, Paul, I needed to hear that. I'll call you soon."

The next day, Paul surprised Madie with another phone call. "Madie, love, I couldn't wait to hear from you. I have to see you again. Please tell me you can meet me in Miami and soon."

She giggled. "Paul, yes, I've worked things out. I can meet you the last week of February."

"Fantastic, luv. Can't wait to see you."

"I know. I can't wait to see you either. I miss you so

much."

"I haven't been able to get you out of my mind. Listen, I'll make all the arrangements at one of the hotels downtown. I'll call you with the details."

"Wonderful. I'll wait to hear from you."

After she hung up the phone, Madie said a silent prayer thanking God for bringing her together with Paul.

The days dragged on and Madie marked each one on her calendar, but knowing that she'd be with him soon, helped. Paul called just days before her departure to let her know he'd pick her up at the airport, and her heart soared. This was happening. This was really happening. She made all her arrangements for the children and made sure she had coverage at work, and told everyone she was headed for a seminar in Miami.

At the airport, Madie collected her luggage and stood where Paul had asked her to wait. She was looking to the right when he came up at her left and wrapped her in a bear hug.

She turned into his embrace and he kissed her hard.

"Paul!" She never knew she had such a shrill squeal hidden inside her.

He picked her up and whirled her around. "I'm so happy to see you again!"

He looked so good to her and he kissed her better and harder than she remembered.

"Let's go to the hotel," he whispered in her ear.

Madie felt the heat suffuse her body and it left her speechless. She could only nod.

Paul had already checked them into the hotel and he led her straight to the room. The suite Paul had booked was big enough for six people. They had barely stepped into the room when Paul began tearing off her clothes. She felt his desire, and it too was stronger than she had remembered.

He kissed her as if he had never kissed her before, and it frightened her, but she felt alive and joyful. He removed his clothes without even stopping for a breath while kissing her. He then carried her to the bed and started kissing her feet and sucking her toes, driving her wild.

He slowly moved up her legs with slow, soft kisses and started licking her thighs. The thought of what was to come made her weak.

"Oh, my Bonnie, how I love you."

She felt as if she would shatter from joy, as his lips explored her most sensitive places. He made her tremble until she exploded in ecstasy. No man had ever taken such pleasure in pleasing her again and again. Part of her pleasure came from watching Paul's expression each time he brought her closer to heaven.

Madie began to cry. It had been such an emotional experience.

"Oh, Madie, please don't cry. What did I do wrong?" He held her tightly.

She sobbed.

"Please calm down." He loosened his arms and held her more gently. "I'm so sorry if I've done something wrong. Please tell me. I'll make it right."

Between sobs she asked, "How could you know my body so well?"

He chuckled. "I think we were lovers in a past life."

Madie laughed.

Paul then said, "How else could we explain that two

people could be this wonderful together?"

She smiled. "Maybe it was destiny." She knew it really didn't make any difference. She only cared that they felt so right together.

Paul let her rest a while then started kissing her neck and slowly moved to her breasts, but she decided it was her turn to drive him crazy. She began by sucking his nipples and he loved this. He gave into everything, and she loved his openness, so unlike her ex-husband.

She explored his body, slowly, luxuriously, sensuously, as never before. She drove him mad with her hands, her tongue, her body, until he could stand it no more. He finally pulled her on top of his body and drove himself so deep inside that she cried out from intense pleasure.

"I love you, Madie!" he shouted as he lost all control.

And Madie joined him in his trek to the stars.

Chapter 5

On their first night together since the Bahamas, they shared hours of lovemaking. As they lay in each others arms exhausted, Madie knew she never wanted to be without Paul. When they had caught their breath, Paul said he wanted to take her dancing to one of his favorite clubs on south beach called Mango's.

He said, "You'll love it, Madie. I want to share everything I love with you."

He was right, and they danced the night away. When they got back to the hotel, Madie felt tired and ready to rest, but Paul had other plans. He had bought some candles and lit them to make the room more romantic

Very slowly, Paul started to remove her clothes. He kissed every newly exposed part of her, sending shivers of anticipation through her.

She allowed Paul to go as far as he wanted. She erected no barriers and he knew it. He continued kissing her, licking her, touching her in all ways until she thought that she'd pass out if he didn't stop.

Eventually, he slid within her and with deep, slow strokes, began to take his pleasure. In a matter of minutes, they both cried out together.

Madie held Paul so closely, she felt the pounding of his heart against her breast. They fell asleep and didn't awake until the next morning.

"It's so nice waking up in your arms," Madie said kissing his ear.

"Mmm. I know exactly what you mean." He rolled away from her and rubbed the sleep from his eyes. He looked at his wristwatch. "Good grief! It's ten o'clock. Time to get up, sleepyhead." He kissed her and headed for the shower.

While Paul showered, Madie called home to check on the children.

"We're fine, Mom. Don't worry about us. So how's the seminar going?"

Madie cleared her throat. "Fine but boring. But you know, I'll get through it."

Satisfied that everything at home was as it should be, Madie called Gia at the office. The conversation went much the same way.

Just then, Paul came out of the bathroom. "By the time you get out of the shower, it'll be nearly time for lunch. Let me take you to a little Cuban restaurant around the corner."

That began a day of new sights and sounds and shopping for Madie as Paul shared his special places with her.

By the end of the day, Paul held her close and looked deeply into her eyes. "Madie, I'm going to marry you, and make a life with you."

Madie felt herself blush down to her toes. She raised her gaze to his and asked, "Paul, are you asking me to marry you?"

A huge grin appeared on his face as he pulled her closer. "Of course I am. What do you say, my Bonnie?"

"Let's make plans."

Paul picked her up and whirled her around. "You've made me the happiest man alive!"

Chapter 6

Back at the hotel, Madie finally had the courage to ask Paul the question that had nagged at her since they had met. "Paul, are you married?"

He took her hand and sat on the bed with her. Madie's heart stopped.

"Yes," he said simply.

"How could you ask me to marry you if you're still married?" Tears welled in Madie's eyes.

He took a deep breath. "We've been separated for over a year and the divorce should be final soon."

Madie felt instantly relieved.

"Madie, do you still love your ex?"

"Not a bit. I'm completely over Patrick. I was very much in love with him at one time, but when he cheated on me, that had killed it. I knew I had to move forward in my life. So, that's why I had filed for my divorce and planned a trip to the Bahamas. Now I'm so happy that I did."

"I'm glad you did too." Then Paul immediately went into planning mode. "I want to see you as much as possible until my divorce becomes a reality, and then we can start our life together."

As any soon-to-be-married couple, they talked of their

plans for the future. Everything was bright, and shiny, and possible.

Later that evening, Paul took Madie to one of his favorite pubs. They ordered drinks and Paul started playing pool with one of the patrons.

Madie watched his every move, and felt totally absorbed in this man she had fallen in love with. As she sat there, she noticed a woman sitting at the table next to hers, staring at her. Madie shifted uncomfortably in her seat. Then the woman moved over to Madie's table and sat across from her.

In heavily accented English, the woman said, "You have beautiful eyes."

Madie shifted her gaze to her drink and said, "Thank you," all the while wishing she'd leave.

"I can see that you have a beautiful soul and spirit."

Madie looked back to Paul hoping he'd return but could see he was totally absorbed in his game.

The woman continued in a honeyed voice. "I can see that you've recently had a lot of pain in your life."

Madie looked back to Paul. This time they made eye contact, and Paul walked over to the table.

"Is everything all right, Madie? Is this woman bothering you?"

With a lack of conviction, Madie said, "I'm fine, Paul."

Then the woman looked from Madie to Paul and back to Madie. "I can see that you're both very happy. How long have you been married?"

"We're not married," Madie said.

She seemed surprised, then said, "Ah, but you will be

one day."

Madie just smiled and Paul went back to playing pool with his newfound buddy.

Then the woman looked at Madie very strangely and tears came from her eyes.

"I'm sorry, are you upset about something?" Madie asked.

She just shook her head. "Ah, you miss your mother, her strength, her love. I'm sorry that you no longer have her with you."

Madie froze. How could this woman have known that her mother had died nearly two years earlier of cancer? She hadn't even told Paul yet.

Paul had seen her sudden change in demeanor and came back over to the table. "Are you sure everything is okay? You look like you've just seen a ghost."

Madie couldn't find the words. Paul turned to the stranger and said, "You've upset my lady here. Please leave."

The woman ignored him and said something that Madie couldn't understand.

"I asked you to leave."

"Paul, I'm fine. Really. Don't let her upset us. Go back to your pool game."

The woman tried again to give her message to Madie, but Madie only shook her head. She had no idea what the woman was trying to tell her.

Paul reached for her hand and helped her up. "Come on, Madie, let's go."

"Paul, I'm fine," she insisted.

Paul led her out of the pub and into the car.

On the drive back to the hotel Paul asked, "What did that woman say to you that upset you so much?"

When Madie told him, he agreed that was more than a bit strange.

"Paul, my mother and I were very close, and when she died, I found it hard to go on. She was my best friend."

At that, Paul pulled the car over and pulled her close to hold her. He didn't say a word. None were needed.

"Madie, I'm so happy to have you in my life. Let me ease the pain for you."

Madie only nodded and they headed back to the hotel.

That night, they lay in each other's arms in a strange calmness. Madie sensed that everything in her life was about to change. The next morning, Madie awoke feeling alive and renewed. Paul called room service and ordered a great breakfast.

"Wow, room service," Madie commented as she got out of bed.

"This is our last day together for a while. I want to spend the whole day in the room. Specifically, in bed."

Madie gave him a seductive smile. That would be fine with me."

Chapter 7

When Madie returned to work, Gia greeted her with all sorts of questions about the seminar. Madie decided to tell her the truth and asked her into her office. With the door shut, Madie told Gia about Paul, their wonderful weekend together, and their plans for the future.

At first Gia seemed a bit upset. "Madie, I can't believe you didn't tell me what was really going on. Why didn't you tell me the truth from the beginning?"

"Gia, you know you would have done the same thing."

Gia glared at her.

"Come on, be honest."

Gia relented, smiled, and nodded.

"Friends?"

Gia said, "Friends," and they embraced. "Thank you for being such a wonderful friend, Gia."

"You're my best friend. What are best friends for? But do you think this long distance relationship stuff is really going to work?"

"It has to. Plus, I think our love is strong enough to maintain a good relationship despite the miles between us, at least until we get married. Once we marry, then of course all that changes."

"I wish you all the best, but if by some chance it doesn't work out for you, you know I'll always be there for you."

"I know that."

"And I'm happy you've found love again."

"Thank you, Gia."

When Gia left the office, Madie sat thinking about Paul and their relationship. She kept telling herself that somehow, it would all work out.

Four days later when Paul called Madie at the office, she thrilled at the sound of his voice, but it sounded as though something was wrong.

"It's nothing, really, and I don't want you to worry. I'm in the hospital."

"Oh, no, Paul, where? What happened?"

"I'm in Miami. I came because I had some chest pains, and frankly, I have a family history of heart disease. The doctors are running some tests, you know these doctors and their tests, but I'll call you when I know the results."

"How about if I come to Miami? Do you need me?"

"No need, luv. Everything will be just fine. You'll see."

Madie tried to keep the rest of the conversation upbeat, but when she hung up the phone, she just shook her head in disbelief. She had just been with him four days ago and he seemed fine.

She whispered a short prayer for his well-being and asked God to always keep him in her life. Two days later, the phone call that she had been waiting for came.

"Paul, it's so good to hear your voice! What did the doctors say?"

"Oh, Bonnie, nothing too dreadful, really. They say I have high blood pressure and mild heart disease. They've prescribed some medications and told me I'd have to change my diet a bit, but it's nothing I can't live with."

"I'm so thankful it wasn't very serious. Please do what the doctors tell you. I want you to stay around for at least another forty years."

He laughed. "I'll be fine. Don't worry so much, or you'll get gray hair like mine."

"I don't care. I love you and your gray hair. I can't wait to see you again."

"My Bonnie, do you think you could get away to meet me next month?"

"Let me check my calendar. I'll let you know as soon as I can pick a date."

"Wonderful. I miss you, you know. I'll be waiting to hear from you about that date."

"Paul, I miss you so much it hurts."

"I know exactly what you mean, luv. I miss you too."

"I'll call you soon."

Chapter 8

Madie and Gia closed out a big deal they had been working on and made quite a bit of money on it. At that point, Madie saw a free spot on her calendar and made plans to meet Paul in Miami. She arranged for her children to stay with their father and asked Gia to check on the kids while she was gone just to make sure everything was fine. A week before her flight, Madie checked her phone messages and heard Paul's voice. At first, she sighed and reveled in the sound of it, then she noted the message.

"Madie, please call before you come. I need to talk to you."

She played it three times. Something was wrong.

She didn't like the sound in his voice, but wasn't sure what it could be about. She immediately called him.

"Paul, I just got your message. Is something wrong?"

"Oh, no, luv. We just need to talk before we meet."

"You have my undivided attention. How about now?"

He cleared his voice. "I don't know how you're going to take this, but I've had to move back in with my soon-to-be ex-wife, because of some financial problems. I just wanted you to know before we met."

The news sent Madie into a tailspin.

"I'm not trying to reconcile with her or anything like that, but I need to save some money, so I don't see that I have much choice."

Numbly, Madie told Paul that she understood.

"Are you truly all right with the situation?" he asked.

"Yes, I'm fine and I understand. I love you. Don't worry. Everything will work out for us."

"I love you too, and I can't wait to see you. You're the best thing that's ever happened to me."

Madie wasn't sure that Paul had told her everything but knew that he would fill her in on all the details when she saw him in Miami.

When Madie walked through the gate at the airport, she found Paul waiting for her. He seemed happy to see her, but distant. He took her luggage then kissed her.

Madie sensed that something had been bothering him but she wasn't sure what.

They made small talk all the way to the hotel and when they arrived at their room, Paul suggested they take a nap.

"I know I'm a bit tired and I'm sure you are too," he said.

"A nap sounds good, but I'd like to unpack first. Why don't you lie down and I'll join you in a few minutes."

He gave her a quick peck on the cheek and made himself comfortable. As Madie put her things away, she didn't like the change she sensed in Paul. He seemed different. She couldn't pinpoint it, but it bothered her tremendously. After she finished unpacking, she lay down beside Paul and drifted off to sleep. When she woke, she found Paul sitting in the chair next to the bed, staring at her. He smiled then sat beside her.

"Paul, I know something's bothering you. Please tell me what it is."

He hesitated a moment and Madie just knew she wasn't going to like what he planned to say.

"Madie, I hate to burden you with this, but while I was in the hospital in Miami, some of my employees stole some money from the business. That's why I'm having my financial problems right now and one of the reasons I've had to move back in with the family. I've never found myself in such a position before and I'm finding it very difficult to deal with.

"I was afraid to say anything to you for fear that you wouldn't want to see me anymore, but I feel I have to be honest with you and that's why I'm telling you everything now."

Madie felt his pain and pulled him close. "Paul, I understand that real life happens and we have to deal with it the best we know how. I couldn't care less if you had one dollar or a million dollars to your name. I love you no matter what. I certainly hope you didn't think I was with you for your money. Did you?"

Paul shook his head. "From experience, I know that all the women I've ever been with have cared whether or not I had money, but you're different. You don't know how much I've worried about how you'd feel when you found out I didn't have as much money as I did when we first met."

Madie looked at him reassuringly. "When we met, I didn't have a clue about how much money you had, and truthfully, the thought never crossed my mind."

Paul pulled her closer.

"Madie, you really do love me for me and nothing else."

She looked deeply into his eyes. "Paul, I've never loved anyone the way I love you, and no amount of money could ever buy my love."

"Madie, I promise. I'm going to do everything I can to build my business back up and make a way for us to have a life together." Now he seemed more at ease, and more like the Paul she remembered. "Can you wait for me to do this?"

"I can wait for you, Paul."

Her words gave him the cue he had been waiting for. He began to kiss her lips and face tenderly, and sighed, "Oh, my Bonnie."

Madie knew exactly what he had in mind, but also felt her stomach rumble with hunger. "Paul, don't you think we need to get something to eat?"

He stopped, looked at her, and laughed. "Oh, my Bonnie, I could live off of you and our love. I don't need anything to eat."

Madie understood exactly what he meant and knew they wouldn't be eating any food that night.

Chapter 9

The next morning, Paul ordered room service for breakfast and seemed in a talkative mood. His conversation revolved around things that had happened in his life, including things he said not even his wife knew, including that he had been involved in drug trafficking at one time and had almost died before he got out.

"I'm not proud of it, but I've managed to straighten myself out and make a better life for myself."

Paul's honesty touched her. "Thank you so much for telling me all this, Paul. I'll never hold your past against you. I know we've all done things that we'd rather not think about, but we make our mistakes and go on."

Paul kissed her. "Oh, Madie, I've never met anyone quite like you."

"And I can assure you that you never will again."

"My, would you look at the time? It's almost five."

"What of it?" Madie asked.

"I've made dinner reservations. Would you like something to eat now, or can you wait until dinner?"

"I can wait until dinner. We had a huge breakfast, and so late."

Madie and Paul took a nap before getting ready for

dinner. As they were about to leave, Paul grabbed her and kissed her as if it were their first time.

With a giggle she pulled away. "Not now, lover. We need to leave if we want to arrive on time for our dinner reservations."

He ignored her and kissed her again.

Playfully, she pushed him away. "If you're a good boy, I can promise you a sweet, lovely little dessert later."

He laughed and led the way to the restaurant.

After dinner, feeling well fed and feeling warm from the wine, Paul and Madie made their way back to their hotel room. Paul paused only briefly to put out the "Do Not Disturb" sign and then smiled at the prospect of Madie's promise of dessert.

The next morning, Madie awoke keenly aware that this would be their last day together for some time. They spent the day at the beach, and their few hours in the sun and sand passed quickly, and they cherished each moment together. They made love that night as if it would be their last, and Madie wept at the prospect of leaving Paul again.

The next morning as Madie packed, she fought hard to hold back the tears.

Paul came up beside her. "Are you all right, luv?"

"No. No, I'm not all right. I've loved these few days with you and now I have to leave. Why can't we just be together?" She broke down in tears.

He hugged her close. "I know. I know. But we'll be together again soon, and permanently. Just remember that. And remember that I love you. The time we manage to spend together will help us through the times ahead. I know, I'm having a hard time letting you go home."

Madie melted into his arms and let him hold her for a few seconds.

"Madie, would you mind taking a taxi to the airport? I have some business to take care of before I leave. I'll understand if you'd rather not, though."

She lied. "That's all right. I can take a taxi. In some ways it'll make saying good-bye easier."

She finished packing and Paul walked her to the lobby. He kissed her good-bye and helped her into the cab.

"I love you. I'll call you soon, luv," he said as the taxi sped away.

Chapter 10

Days later, Paul finally called Madie.

"Paul, where've you been? I've been trying to call you. I haven't heard from you. What's going on?"

"Oh, Madie, luv. That's just it. There's so much going on with me, and I really can't discuss it over the phone."

"Paul, you're scaring me. Something's very wrong. I can hear it in your voice."

"Nothing I can't handle, luv. You'll just have to trust me."

"Don't you know you can tell me anything?"

"I know that, luv, but I've got to go to court over the next month or two, and we'll have to wait to meet until July."

"Court? July? Paul, that's so far away? And why haven't you called me before now? I've been worried sick about you."

"I can't talk about it now, but I'll tell you everything when next I see you."

The tone in his voice told her that he was trying to tell her something, but she wasn't sure what.

Almost dissolving into tears, Madie said, "I love you. I'll be here when you call again. Please just take care of yourself."

"I will, luv. Don't worry so much about me. I'll be fine. Everything will work out. You'll see. I promise. I'll call you soon."

The click on the phone sounded so final, and Madie suddenly felt a large, hollow spot in her chest.

Two weeks passed without a word from Paul. Madie threw herself into her work and children, all the time wondering about her lover.

Just when she thought she was at her lowest, Gia walked into her office and made an announcement.

"Madie, get yourself a babysitter. You're coming with me tonight. I know this great little club I used to go to all the time, and you'll love it."

"But, I can't."

"Yes, you can. I'm tired of seeing you mope around here. You need to have some fun."

"I'm not moping," Madie protested.

"Yeah, right."

"Okay, I'll go with you, but not because I'm moping, but because I just need to relax."

Madie and Gia hadn't been there very long before Gia had her laughing hard at one of her jokes. Clearly, Madie needed a night out to relax and have fun. Yet, as she continued to think about Paul, she wished she could get her mind on someone or something else.

As if on cue, a dark haired gentleman walked over to their table. Gia flashed him a huge smile. Madie barely look up at him.

"Excuse me, ladies. I hope you're having a wonderful evening."

"We're having a great time. How about you?" Gia answered.

"A lovely evening." Then he smiled at Madie. "I was wondering if you'd like to dance with me, lovely lady?"

A bit flustered, Madie looked at Gia who smiled her approval. Madie smiled back then turned to her mysterious gentleman.

"Yes, I'd like to dance with you."

He took her hand and led her to the dance floor.

"So what's your name?" he asked as he positioned himself at a respectable distance.

"My friends call me Madie. And you are?"

"You can call me Don. You know, I saw you when you walked in, and I've been watching you all evening. I think you're exceptionally beautiful. I can't believe you agreed to dance with me."

Madie flushed at the compliment. "Thank you for saying so." She tried not to carry on too much of a conversation with him, because she didn't want him to think that she was available.

"I'm a cardiologist. I just love to come here to unwind once in a while. What do you do for a living?"

"Don, I appreciate the dance but I don't think it's appropriate to discuss what I do for a living."

"So sorry, Madie. I didn't mean to pry. I was just trying to make conversation."

"I don't want you to think I'm rude or anything, but I'm in a relationship and I just don't feel comfortable sharing that information with you."

"I understand," he said. "Then would you have dinner with me this Friday?"

Madie gave him a puzzled look. "No, I'm sorry, no. I'm seeing someone."

"You misunderstand me. I don't want to romance you. I'd just like to get to know you as a friend."

Madie wasn't quite sure how to take his intentions, but sensed his sincerity. "I'll think about it, okay?"

"Fair enough."

He escorted her back to her table and handed her one of his cards. "Please let me know about Friday night. Call me."

"Thank you for the dance, and the card. I'll think about it."

He smiled and left her to Gia.

"You'll think about it. What's wrong with you? He's gorgeous! He's a doctor!"

Madie just gave Gia a silent look.

"If you ask me, and you didn't, but if you did, I'd tell you that you'd be a fool to pass up a man like that, especially for somebody like Paul, and you and I know you'll probably never see him again."

Without a word, Madie started to gather her things.

"Where are you going?" Gia asked.

"Home. We're about to have our first fight and I don't want it to be here."

Gia grabbed her purse and threw a tip down on the table before following Madie out the door.

"Madie, I know you're in love with Paul, but you don't exactly have a ring and a date. Plus the guy has moved back in with his soon-to-be-ex. What does that tell you? You need to see somebody else. Paul's not the only fish in the sea, you know."

Madie stopped as she reached her car and turned to her friend. "Look, I appreciate you worrying about me, but I love Paul too much to think about any other man. As my friend, you can support me or not. It's up to you."

Gia shrugged her shoulders in resignation. "Neither one of us is going to convince the other, so I'll just leave it alone. I'll see you at the office tomorrow. Okay? Friends?"

"Friends."

They gave each other a sisterly embrace and parted.

On her way home, Madie's thoughts drifted to Paul, to Don, then back to Paul. She wished Paul were with her. She thought about Don and how handsome he was. She wasn't sure they could be friends, or was this just his way of getting into her life. She found herself wishing that life and love were simpler.

Madie's office phone rang soon after she arrived.

"Madie here."

"My, Bonnie."

The words, the voice sent jolts of emotion through her and she settled into her chair.

"Paul, what a nice surprise!"

"Just calling to see how you're doing, and to let you know that it may be as late as August or September before I can meet you again."

"Oh, Paul, I don't like the sound of that, but I suppose we have to deal with it. But you must promise to let me know the earliest date you can get away."

"You know I will. Madie, is everything all right?"

"Absolutely. I'm fine. I just miss you so."

"I love you, Madie."

"I love you, too."

"I'll call you soon."

Madie had a feeling that something was terribly wrong. "Paul, if you need to tell me something, you know you can."

"What can possibly be wrong?"

"I don't know. You just don't sound right," Madie insisted.

"I'm fine. Just tired. Listen, I've got to go. Love you. Call you soon."

"Before she had a chance to answer, the phone went dead. She hoped he'd call back, but the call never came.

Two weeks passed with no word from Paul. She knew something was wrong, and it was probably that he had tired of her. Maybe Gia had been right. Maybe she should see other people. She rummaged through her purse and found the card that Don had given her. For the first time she read the card that said Dr. Don Shaver, specializing in cardiovascular surgery. Maybe they could be friends.

When she called him, he sounded very surprised. "Madie, so glad you called. Do you have a restaurant in town that you prefer?"

"No anyplace would be fine, really. Casual. Friends. Remember?"

"Absolutely. Friends. Now, if you give me your number, I can call to let you know place and time. Or I could pick you up."

Madie gave him her number. "Just let me know where, Don, and I'll meet you there."

Madie did not tell Gia about her plans to meet Don for dinner and on Friday afternoon, Don called as promised. "Meet you at seven at Mario's restaurant. Nice family place. Casual, but fun. Good people there. Here's my beeper number in case you need to reach me."

That evening, as Madie drove to the restaurant, she couldn't help but feel a little nervous. She thought about Paul far too much. When she arrived, she found Don waiting for her. He greeted her as she came through the door. Madie couldn't help thinking how handsome he was.

"Madie, I don't know how it's possible, but you're more beautiful than the night I met you."

Madie only blushed.

"I'm so glad you decided to meet me tonight."

"Me too," she said shyly.

"Two for dinner?" the hostess asked.

"Yes, non smoking, please." He turned to Madie, "Is that alright?"

She nodded.

As the hostess led the way to the table, Madie wondered why she had chosen to meet Don. She was in love with Paul. She felt like a cheat.

After they had ordered their meal, Don tried to make small talk. "You'll love the veal Parmesan. They do a very good job of it here. Next time, you'll have to try the veal and peppers. In fact, you can have some from my plate tonight."

"I look forward to it, Don." Madie shifted in her seat uncomfortably.

"So what made you decide to call me?"

She made no mention of Paul. Instead, she gave him the highlights of her family and divorce, hoping to satisfy his curiosity.

"You mentioned you were seeing someone. Is that

someone the reason for your divorce?" Don wanted to know.

"Oh, no, not at all. My husband had a penchant for extracurricular activities."

"May I ask who you're seeing?"

"You may ask, but that's personal. I don't feel comfortable talking with you about my love life."

He quickly changed the subject to something else and they finished dinner.

As Don walked her to her car, he asked, "May I see you again, Madie?"

"I'm not sure. I'll have to think about it, but if I decide to, you'll be the first to know. Thank you for a wonderful dinner and the conversation."

As she turned to get into her car, he startled her with a kiss on the cheek. "I'm sorry," Don said. "I just had to do that. You look so lovely in the moonlight."

"Don't worry about it. I'm just tired and need to go home.

"If, in the future, you want to have dinner with a friend, give me a call."

Madie nodded and left. She still thought about Paul and how things were going for him, but she also had to admit she had enjoyed her evening with Don. She also reminded herself to take care with this man, because she had a feeling he wanted more than she did.

Chapter 11

By the middle of May, Madie had not heard anything from Paul yet, and her anxiety level doubled. She had tried several times to call his office but had not reached him.

She kept herself occupied with work as much as possible, but often found her concentration waning because all she could think about was Paul. In the meantime, Don called her at least once a week and asked to have dinner with her. She turned him down every time. She felt she needed to keep him at a distance, but maybe just one more dinner would be fine.

"Yes, yes! Dinner Friday night would be wonderful. Shall I make reservations for us at Mario's again?"

"That would be fine. I'll call you on Friday about noon just to confirm that we're still on," Madie told him.

"Sounds good to me. See you then."

On Friday evening, Don arrived about fifteen minutes late.

"Sorry, I'm late. I had an emergency.

He just looked too handsome and too well composed to have just come from an emergency, but Madie didn't mention it. "That's quite alright, Don. You called to let me know. You're a doctor. I don't mind."

Though he thanked her for her understanding, he seemed nervous.

They ordered dinner and Don told her about a patient he had seen that afternoon. "She almost died, but we caught it in time. She, and of course her family, were all so grateful. But truth be told, I was too. I was just happy to be at the right place at the right time for her."

"I hope she's going to be alright," Madie said with concern.

"Oh, yeah, she's going to pull through beautifully."

During that dinner, Don seemed to talk about everything that had ever happened to him, and it annoyed her. She had never thought of Don as so self-centered.

Finally he asked about her relationship.

"Just fine, and if I want to share the particulars with you, I'll let you know. It's still not a subject I care to discuss."

He accepted her comment and told her about his two children.

"So why did you divorce?" Madie asked.

"My ex hated that I was a doctor and that it took so much of my time. She loved me once, but came to hate the hours and late night emergencies. It takes a very special woman to be a doctor's wife, but my ex and I are still very good friends."

He continued to talk about his children, and Madie could see that he truly loved them.

When they had finished their meal, Madie said, "Thank you for dinner, Don, but I'm tired and need to call it a day."

"Can I see you again tomorrow night?"

Madie thought a moment. "My son has a late afternoon soccer game tomorrow. We'll both be a bit tired after that. Maybe sometime soon. Can I take a rain check?"

"Well, I'm sorely disappointed but I understand. The kids always come first."

Don walked her to her car and kissed her cheek.

"Thanks again, Don. I'll call when I know I can get away for dinner again."

"Make it soon, Madie. I so enjoy your company."

During the next week, Don called three times asking Madie to dinner but she turned him down. Paul still had not called so she decided to write him. The following week Don called again but she still turned him down.

At the end of the next week, Gia walked into Madie's office crying and Madie immediately rose from her desk and went to console her friend.

"What's wrong, Gia?"

"My father has had a heart attack and they don't know if he's going to make it."

"Well, you have to go to him," Madie insisted.

"I know I need to leave right away. But I was working on this deal."

"Don't give it another thought. Just leave the file out on your desk and I'll take care of it. You go home and pack. I'll make your flight arrangements for you."

"Would you, please?"

"Yes, now go. I'll call you and pick you up at your place and take you to the airport."

"Thanks, Madie."

"That's what friends are for. Now go!"

Madie booked an early afternoon flight for her friend

and got her to the airport on time. On her way back, she decided to stop by Don's office.

The place looked like any other doctor's office and only a few seconds had elapsed when the receptionist asked, "May I help you?"

"Yes, I'm a friend of Don's. I was just wondering if he had a few moments to see me."

Just then, Don walked up to the front desk and looked very surprised to see her. "Madie, so glad you came by. Come on back to my office." He led her down the hall and offered a chair. "I'll just be a few minutes. I'm just finishing up with a patient."

While she waited, she studied Don's degrees hanging on the wall and thought them a very impressive collection of degrees. She looked at his office décor and thought some of his choices quite surprising. Don walked in about fifteen minutes later.

"So to what do I owe the honor and pleasure?" he asked as he sat behind his desk.

Madie told him about Gia's father and that she had decided to stop by on her way back from the airport because she had a few minutes to spare. She had just been so busy lately.

"That was very nice of you. Do you have any other time to spare for dinner?" He gave her a fantastic, hopeful smile.

"I'd love to, but that's nearly impossible right now with Gia gone, but I'll certainly consider it when she gets back."

They talked a few more minutes and Madie stood to leave. "Look, I know you're busy and I've got to get back to the office, but I'll call you soon."

"I look forward to it."

Madie offered her hand and Don tenderly shook it. She just didn't know what to make of this man.

That night, Gia called. Madie, thanks again for all your help. I just wanted you to know that my Dad's stable, but not terrific, but stable."

"Well, that's better than his condition this morning," Madie comforted.

"I think he's gonna make it. I can feel it in my bones. Oh, Madie, please tell me he's gonna make it," she pleaded.

Madie sighed. "Of course he's going to make it. He's strong. He'll make it. Besides, how can he leave when he still has to keep an eye on you?"

Gia allowed herself a little chuckle. "Thanks, friend. Oh, by the way, did you find that file?"

"Yep, and I'm working it. Don't worry about it. You just take care of things there and let me know if you need anything. And make sure you keep me updated on your dad's condition."

"Will do, and thanks again."

Madie knew that Gia's father's condition was very serious. She hoped for the best, but prepared herself for the worst. Gia would need her if he worsened and died.

Her thoughts immediately went to Paul. What if he were ill? What if he had died? That would explain why he hadn't called. On the other hand, he may be having second thoughts about the two of them.

On Friday, Madie called Don.

"What a delightful surprise! I'm so glad you called. Please tell me you're calling because you'd like to see me," he said.

Madie giggled. "As a matter of fact I am. I thought maybe we could have a quick light dinner tonight, but I need to be home early."

"Wonderful. Any time I can spend with you I will. I can be at your office about 5:30 if that works for you."

"Absolutely doable," she said. "I'll see you later."

As Madie hung up the phone, she found herself questioning why she had called him. Why did she want to see him? The little alarm bells were going off in her head but she shut them off and went back to her work.

Don came by the office as he said he would and Madie followed him to one of his favorite restaurants. They shared a wonderful dinner and Don didn't seem as self-engrossed as before. After dinner, he escorted her back to her car and tried to kiss her on the lips, but she turned her head, and his lips landed on her cheek.

"Don, I thought we agreed not to share anything but friendship, and that doesn't include kissing." She felt like a schoolteacher reprimanding a naughty little boy. "I'm surprised you even tried."

"I'm sorry, Madie. You're just so beautiful, I find it hard to control myself."

"Don, you've made your attraction for me very clear, on more than one occasion, but we agreed to remain just friends. If we can't stick to that agreement, then we shouldn't see each other again."

"Oh, no, Madie, I have to see you again. I promise I won't try anything like that again. Please call me again."

Madie said nothing for a few seconds. "I'll think about it. Thank you for dinner tonight. I have to get home."

During the next few days Gia informed Madie of her father's improvement and that she'd stay with him until he went home from the hospital. "Would that be a problem for you, Madie?'

"Of course not, stay as long as you need to. I just hope he'll be okay," Madie told her.

"I know this will put a lot more work on you," Gia said.

"Don't worry about it. The work will keep my mind occupied and I won't think about Paul so much."

That week Don called several times asking to see her, and she turned him down each time. She still felt a little anger about her last dinner with him.

Each time she turned him down he said, "I'm so disappointed, but rest assured I won't give up. One of these days you'll say yes. I can wait for that day. I'm a patient man."

That last little statement made the alarms go off again in her head, but she chalked it up to his innate arrogance, and went on with her life.

By the second week in June, Madie still had no word from Paul, and she began to really worry. She tried not to think something bad had happened to him, but couldn't shake the feeling that something was very wrong. She even contemplated going to the Bahamas to try to find him, but she couldn't leave right now. She could only sit and wait.

And then maybe all her worry was for nothing. Maybe he had only reconciled with his wife. When she considered all the possibilities, it made her head hurt.

Chapter 12

With Gia gone, Madie found herself working ten to twelve hour days, and she felt close to exhaustion. Though her children tried to hide it, they hated that she was gone so much, and that upset her.

By the end of June, Madie found herself wishing that Gia would come back to work. She had still not heard from Paul, and she couldn't stop wondering why he hadn't called. Don had begun to call on a regular basis, and she continued to turn down his invitations to dinner and other events. Gia finally returned during the second week of July and it seemed that life would return to normal for Madie. When it seemed that Gia had gotten back into the swing of things, she told Gia she'd like to take a few days off.

"Sure, go ahead. You need a few days off. You've been doing double duty for far too long. I really appreciate that you let me stay away so long while my dad recovered from his heart attack. Now it's your turn. Go ahead. Go to the Bahamas or something."

Madie couldn't help smiling. "I just might do that, Gia. Thanks." And that's exactly what she did.

When Madie stepped out of the Bahamian airport, she took a moment to enjoy the warm sun on her face. Memories of her time here with Paul flooded her. She shook off the melancholy that threatened and looked for the car that the hotel had sent. She spotted it in a moment and immediately recognized Carl, the driver.

He smiled at her as she approached. "So good to see you again and that you're back on the island. Is your friend with you?"

"No, actually, I'm alone this time."

"Well, if you need anything during your stay, let me know. I'm at your service."

"Thank you, Carl. May I have another one of your cards?"

"Gladly, Miss." He reached into his breast pocket and handed me a card. "Now don't hesitate to call if you need me."

"Thank you, you're very kind."

After Madie checked in at the hotel and took her luggage to her room, she tried to figure where to start her search for Paul. She decided to go to the club where she first met him, hoping that he might be there. She stayed until closing, but he never showed up. Sorely disappointed, she returned to her room for a restless night's sleep.

The next morning she went to where she thought Paul's business was located but didn't find any sign of it. Confused and concerned, she asked a few of the nearby merchants if they knew of Paul's business, but no one knew anything about a Paul Nobles.

Madie grew more confused than ever. She knew Paul had given her this address. Now she began to wonder about the truth of anything he had told her. She decided to go back to the hotel and page Carl to see if he might be able to help her. Carl returned her page quickly and after she asked him about Paul, he said he knew nothing about him and that he was sorry he couldn't help me.

With only one more day left to find Paul, her frustration level grew. She decided to go back to the club that night for one more try. It was, after all, one of his regular haunts, and she felt that if he were on the island, he'd eventually show up there.

She went to all the places they had gone to together, hoping to find him, but to no avail. She hit a dead end with each attempt. Her thoughts dwelled on Paul and of their time together. He had made her feel so loved. Now she only felt alone. But now, it seemed as if Paul had fallen off the face of the earth and she wondered if he had just used her. Quickly, she pushed that thought away and dressed for her evening at the club.

She again left feeling disappointed when Paul failed to arrive. Back in her room, she couldn't help feeling that she had had wasted three days looking for Paul. But then, she figured that maybe it wasn't meant to be. He had probably reconciled with his wife and chalked up their relationship to one of those romantic flings that meant little in the grand scheme of things.

The next morning, Madie packed her things and took her flight home. When she got back home that afternoon, her children jumped up and down with happiness and hugged her.

"How was your trip, Mom?"

"What did you bring me?"

"Did you make any new friends?"

Madie told them all about her weekend in the mountains, and that there weren't any stores around to buy anything, and that she didn't make any new friends. She kept pretty much to herself and relaxed by the pool. She hated to lie to them, but felt she didn't have a choice. How could she tell them that she had gone on a fruitless journey to find a lover who had disappeared? She did a good job of appearing happy and rested, and only when they had all gone to bed did Madie allow herself the luxury of tears, of disappointment, of frustration. If she ever wanted to be happy again, she'd have to put Paul and the Bahamas behind her forever. The question was, did she have the strength to do that? Did she want to do that?

The next week, Madie got back into her routine and threw herself into her work and her family. She dared not tell anyone where she had gone, what she had done, or what she was feeling.

Then Don called. "Madie, I haven't seen you in so long. I know I'm probably going to be turned down again, but I'd really like to see you. Let me take you to dinner."

Madie hesitated for less than a heartbeat. "Sure, Don. Let's go to dinner. Friends should get together once in a while."

Don took in a deep breath. "I understand exactly what you mean. How about Saturday night? I have a meeting at the hospital late on Friday and Lord only knows how late it will go."

"Saturday will do just fine. Shall we meet at The Rose Arbor?"

"Wonderful choice! Shall we say at seven?"

"Seven it is."

When Madie arrived at the restaurant that evening, the hostess called her by name. "You must be Madie."

"Why, yes."

"Please follow me to your table."

Bewildered, Madie followed the young woman to the back of the restaurant where Don sat. When he saw her approach, he stood to greet her. "Madie, you look more beautiful every time I see you."

His comment made her a bit uncomfortable but she thanked him and sat in the chair he held for her.

Don tried making small talk, but very quickly saw that the conversation bored her. After a brief, uneasy silence, Don asked the question that Madie hoped would never come.

"Madie, I'd really like to date you. You know, see you romantically. I think about you all the time and this friendship thing isn't really working for me. But if it's all I can get, then I suppose I'll take it. But it seems to me that you're very unhappy, so whatever you're doing right now, or whomever you're seeing isn't working. Maybe it's time for a change. Maybe you should give me a chance to make you happy."

His words reached right into her heart and Madie wanted to break down and cry. Instead, she steeled herself against the truth. "Why, Don, I'm very happy. Really. But, I've thought about you too. I'll think about dating you romantically."

Don's face lit up like a hundred-watt light bulb.

"Madie, even the possibility makes me so very happy."

Madie smiled and excused herself. In the restroom, she broke down and took a long look at herself in the mirror. A woman came in behind her, and noticing her tears, stopped to offer advice.

Her bangle bracelets jangled as she draped her arm across Madie's shoulders. "Honey, I can see you're all tore up about some man. Ain't no man I know of worth that much pain. Put him behind you and get on with living. I can tell you that from experience." She gave an emphatic nod and left Madie to her heartbreak.

A minute later, the woman returned to see Madie wiping her tears and freshening her makeup. The woman smiled brightly and said, "That's it, honey. Get on out there and get on with it."

Madie turned and touched the woman's arm before she left. "Thank you. I needed to hear that from someone else."

"No problem. We women gotta stick together."

In the mirror, Madie watched the woman leave. "Yep, we women gotta stick together," she echoed.

Back at the table, Madie put thoughts of Paul behind her while she made small talk with Don. After diner, Don walked her to her car, but this time he didn't try to kiss her, for which Madie felt very thankful.

She hugged him and thanked him for the dinner and told him that she'd call him soon. By the time she arrived home, her loneliness for Paul had blossomed but knew she couldn't do much about it. She'd have to wait until he called her. She'd just have to hold on to the thought that he would.

By the first week of August, Paul had still not called, and Don had stopped calling. Madie supposed he was either hoping she'd call or that he was tired of being turned down.

Just about that time, Gia asked Madie to go with her to their favorite blues club. Madie decided she needed some fun and agreed. They danced a few dances, drank a few drinks, and had a good time together.

"Gia, I'm so glad you asked me to come with you tonight. I've had so much fun. Sometimes I think I've almost forgotten how to have fun."

That night, after checking with her children, Madie went home with Gia because her house was closer and Madie had had a little too much to drink. She enjoyed a much needed sound sleep that night, and when she woke the next morning, she heard movement in the kitchen. Madie got herself out of bed and padded down the hall where she saw Gia sitting at the kitchen table nursing a cup of coffee.

"Mornin'. How'd you sleep?" Gia lifted her cup as if in a toast.

Madie ran a hand through her hair. "Slept great. Need coffee."

Gia laughed and went to the stove. She poured a cup of java and placed it on the table. "Sugar and milk are right there."

Madie sat at the chair and began mixing her coffee.

Gia took a gulp from her cup then put it down in front of her. "Madie, I think we're pretty good friends, if not best friends. You just seem preoccupied, or as if something is wrong. Do you have anything you want to talk about?"

Madie took a sip of her coffee. "You know me too well, Gia. Yes, something's wrong. Paul has disappeared."

"Disappeared? What?"

Madie explained her relationship with Paul and about her secret trip to the Bahamas with him and then in search of him. "Gia, I don't know what's happened to him. He hasn't called or written. I'm afraid something terrible has happened."

"Oh, Madie, I'm so sorry, but these long distance romances are bogus if you ask me. Never a good idea. I hate to see you hurt so much. How can I help?"

"I don't know of anything you can do. In fact, I don't know of anything anyone can do. I guess I just have to keep hoping for the best. I'm not ready to give up on Paul yet."

Gia pouted.

"Now what's wrong with you?" Madie asked.

"I'm hurt that you didn't trust me enough to tell me about your trip to the Bahamas."

"Yeah, and if I had, you probably would've tried to keep me from going. Please understand that I felt I had to go to try to find Paul."

Madie and Gia discussed all sorts of possibilities about Paul until late morning when Madie finally left for home. She spent the day cleaning, cooking, getting ready for the upcoming week, and playing with her children. Late that night the phone rang. She hated when the phone rang so late at night because it usually meant bad news.

"Hello."

No answer.

"Hello. Is anybody there?"

No answer.

She hung up thinking it was probably a wrong number. Unable to sleep, she spent some time writing in her journal and fell asleep thinking of Paul.

The next day, she took the children to church and then out to lunch. By coincidence she ran into Don at the restaurant. Madie and the children had just given their order when Don walked over to the table.

"Hello, Madie. What a nice surprise to see you here," he said. "You're looking lovely as usual."

"Thank you, Don. It's good to see you too."

"I see you've got plenty of company with you," he chuckled and winked at the children.

"Don, these are my children."

"Yes, you've talked so much about them, I feel as though I know them. Hi, kids. My name is Don and I'm a friend of your Mom's."

"Hi, Don," they said in shy unison.

"Well, I won't keep you. I'll let you get back to your meal. See you, Madie. Give me a call sometime."

Madie and the children watched as Don left money on the table and left the restaurant.

"Mom, who is that?" they wanted to know.

"Just an acquaintance. Someone I met at work. Hey, you guys better save room for dessert. They have all sorts of scrumptious things here."

The children then began chattering about chocolate cake and apple pie, for which Madie was thankful. She didn't want to talk anymore about Don, but come tomorrow, she'd be sure to call him and let him know she didn't appreciate that he had invaded her time with her family.

The next day, Madie did as she had planned and called Don at his office.

"Madie, good to hear from you. Quite a surprise to see

you yesterday."

"Yes, and that's exactly why I'm calling. I didn't appreciate you coming over to our table and introducing yourself to my children."

"Madie, I can tell you're terribly upset about this. Why does it bother you so much?"

"Lots of reasons. The divorce has been hard on these kids and I don't want them to think that some strange man is about to step into their father's place. I don't need them asking questions. I didn't appreciate it."

"Madie, I'm so sorry. I didn't mean to make the wrong impression. As far as they're concerned, we're just friends."

"As far as either one of us is concerned, we're both friends."

"Again, I sincerely apologize. Please forgive me. Please tell me this isn't the end of our friendship, that I can see you again."

"Maybe, at some point, but right now I'm just so upset I can't even think about it." She hung up the phone before he could say anything else.

She felt a little guilty for her abruptness with Don, but she had to make her position clear.

Chapter 13

The next week, Don invited Madie to his place for dinner. She wasn't sure if she should accept, but she was feeling pretty low and needed some upbeat company, so she accepted.

She arrived at Don's house about 6:30 that Friday evening and found that he had cooked a beautiful meal. He had placed fresh flowers and candles on the table. He had obviously taken a lot of time preparing this meal.

"Don, this looks beautiful. Thank you for going to so much trouble."

As it turned out, Don was a great cook and the dinner was fabulous. She ate until she thought she'd burst. After dinner, he put a CD in his CD player and he struck up a conversation.

"Don, I think I finally feel comfortable enough with you to tell you about Paul. I think you need to know."

Madie told him about Paul, how they met, and how he had just disappeared from her life.

"Madie, I appreciate your honesty, and I'm flattered that you feel comfortable with me now. But if you let me, I can make you forget about Paul. If you just give us a chance, I know we can build a life together. Your kids already like me."

Don's words made her feel strange, but she recognized the truth of what he said. She needed to move on with her life and Don might prove to be just what she needed. He always treated her kindly, gently, and she found herself beginning to really like him. After some conversation and a few glasses of wine, Don pulled her close. She pulled back.

"Don, I think we need to take this very slowly. I'm still hurting."

"I understand. Take all the time you need to get him out of your system."

"Thank you, Don. I really do appreciate your understanding." She glanced at her watch. "Would you look at the time? I really need to be getting home."

"Fine, Madie. Whatever you want."

Once home, she wrote in her journal, and recorded all her feelings and frustrations. She had to sort this all out.

Little by little, Madie started to see Don on a regular basis and felt herself growing closer to him, but thoughts of Paul still haunted her. What had happened to him?

Now nearly December, she had not yet heard from Paul and decided to write him again as a last resort. She felt she had to make one last try before she gave up on him.

She poured her heart out in that letter. She asked why he had not called or written. She told him of her concern for him and that she was just about ready to give up on him. She told him about Don and begged Paul to call her soon.

Madie sent the letter the next day praying Paul would receive her letter before Christmas. In the meantime, she continued to see Don and knew his patience was nearly at an end.

Chapter 14

Christmas came and went, and Madie had still heard no word from Paul. Don made plans for himself and Madie to spend New Year's Eve at a small bed and breakfast Inn he had read about. Her children wanted to stay with their father for the New Year holiday, so this worked out perfectly.

They had a wonderful time and little by little, Madie was beginning to need Don in her life. He did everything he could to make her forget Paul, and he was beginning to succeed.

When they returned to Boston, Don found out that his mother had passed away and he needed to leave immediately to help with her funeral arrangements. His father, though still alive, suffered from Alzheimer's disease and couldn't handle the details. He asked Madie to take him to the airport and on the way asked Madie the question she had been avoiding.

"Madie, have you given any more thought to becoming my wife?"

Madie blinked back sudden tears and shook her head. "No, Don. I really haven't and I'm not sure we should even talk about it right now. Your mother has just passed away and you've got so much on your mind."

He let out a huge sigh.

"Tell you what. I'll think about it while you're away. Fair enough?"

Don nodded.

"I'll give you an answer when you get back."

Over the next week while Don was gone, he called nearly every day to express his love. Madie felt as if the walls were closing in on her. She wasn't ready to commit to anyone, but she tried to keep the conversation upbeat. After all, he had enough to contend with at the moment.

Despite all the little red flags that went up in her head, she began to think that she should accept this man's offer of love and a future.

A week after he had left, Don returned home and called Madie.

"How are you, Darling?"

"Fine. Did you have a good flight?"

"No problems. I've been missing you. No, I miss you desperately. I want to see you."

"You sound tired."

"I am. What with the funeral, and taking care of Dad, and the estate, and everything. I think I could sleep for a week. With Mom gone, I've had to hire someone to stay with Dad. What a mess. I know that can't go on forever, but I guess I'll just take things as they go."

"Get a good night's rest, Don."

"Yeah, you too. But I'll be all rested up by tomorrow. Can I see you after work tomorrow?"

"Call me at lunch and I'll let you know what time I can meet you."

"Wonderful."

She heard the smile in his voice.

"Goodnight, Darling."

"Goodnight."

"Until tomorrow."

Madie hung up the phone knowing she'd have to have an answer for him when she saw him. She spent a sleepless night, tossing and turning, exploring the possibilities.

The next day, Don called and they set a date for 6:30. Now she felt her back truly pressed against the wall.

When she hung up the phone, Gia waltzed into her office.

"Must have been Don," she said sitting in a chair in front of Madie's desk.

"Yeah, how can you tell?"

"I can see the look on your face."

Madie shrugged.

"So are you going to marry the dude or not?"

"I don't know."

"You should, you know. The dude's a doctor. He's got money. You'd have some kind of security for yourself and the kids."

"But is that any reason to marry him? Is that any reason to marry anyone?"

"Marry him." Gia got up to leave.

"I might, but you know it's still none of your business."

Gia smiled. "I know, but you know me. I love putting my nose in other people's business."

"You'll be the first to know," Madie said sarcastically.

Gia left the office with a smile and Madie got down to

making her final decision on Don's proposal. She spent the afternoon talking to herself. She knew Don was a good man and he would treat her well, but she still found herself thinking of Paul. That would have to stop, but something just didn't feel right. She had an uneasy feeling.

She met Don as planned and he took her to one of their favorite restaurants.

"You still look tired," Madie observed.

"I didn't sleep real well last night. I'll be better tomorrow."

"Well, maybe we should make it an early night," Madie suggested.

"Madie, I have something to talk to you about. Since this all happened, I've thought about moving my practice closer to my family. With only my sister and myself to take care of Dad, I really don't want to put the entire burden on her."

"Move, what that's nearly 500 miles away. This is a surprise." Madie could have kicked herself for being so selfish. She reminded herself to have some understanding for Don and his situation.

"I can move my practice without any problem. I can work anywhere. I'm a doctor."

He studied her a moment. "I suppose you can guess what's coming next. If I move my practice, I'll want to do it soon, and in that case, I'd want to marry you soon as well. What do you say, Madie?"

"Wow, this is a lot to digest. Don, I've thought about this a long time, and I do want to marry you, but I don't want to move. If the move is part of the mix, then I'm afraid I have to say no. I've got my work here. The children are in school here. Their father lives here. I can't just pick up and go."

Don silently nodded. "I understand, Madie."

He motioned for the waitress. "Check please. If you don't mind, I'd like to go home now."

Madie nodded. She saw the hurt and disappointment in his eyes and knew she had put it there. She felt terrible, but could not accept his proposal.

The next morning, Don called her before she left the house.

"Good morning, Madie, I'd like to take you to lunch. I need to talk with you."

She hesitated.

"Please, Madie, it's important."

"All right. Let's meet at the deli down the street from my office. I'll see you at noon?"

"Noon it is."

Madie hung up the phone wondering what in the world Don could possibly have to say.

Madie got to the deli at noon, but Don hadn't arrived yet, which she thought strange. She ordered a sandwich and about fifteen minutes later, her cell phone rang. Don's office number flashed at her.

"Madie, I had an emergency. I've just finished up. If you could wait about 30 more minutes, I'll be there. Will you wait?"

"Sure, I'll wait. I'll order for you."

The waitress brought his sandwich just as Don arrived.

He kissed her cheek and took the seat opposite her. "Thanks for meeting me like this. Thanks for waiting." He took a bite of his sandwich then told her about the patient he had just treated.

"Madie, I've thought a lot about our conversation last night. I really want to marry you, so I've decided not to move back home."

"Don, I don't want to be the reason you stay. You have to make that decision independent of me. You have to make sure this is what you really want."

"Madie, I assure you, I'm not staying just for you. I really don't want to move back home. It was just an idea I had amidst all the sorrow and confusion of the funeral."

"If you're sure. If you're not staying just for me, then yes, let's get married."

He jumped up from his seat, picked her up, and spun her around, right there in the middle of the deli.

"You've made me the happiest man in the world."

Madie smiled and cried, but the tears stemmed from a feeling that she had betrayed Paul. But now she'd have to leave him far behind her.

Back at the office, Madie found Gia standing at the front desk.

"Gia, would you come into my office? I'd like to talk with you."

Looking puzzled, she followed Madie into her office and shut the door behind her. "Is something wrong?"

"No, nothing is wrong. I just wanted to tell you that I've agreed to marry Don."

"No! Yes! No! You didn't! You did!" She screamed. "Congratulations! Can I be your maid of honor?"

"Of course. Who else?"

"Got a date?"

"We thought June would be nice. We just have to

settle on a date."

"That's wonderful! I wish you both all the best in the world. That's fantastic! I'm going to block out the whole month of June, and May too for that matter! There's just so much to do!" Gia squealed one more time and headed for her phone.

Madie only shook her head. How could anyone so smart be so goofy?

Now the end of January, it had been nearly a year since she had heard from Paul. She had officially let go of him, but felt she needed to write to tell him she planned to marry Don. She didn't even know if he was still alive, but she felt she owed him that much.

That night, she gathered up all her courage and started to write.

Dear Paul,

I hope this letter finds you in good health. I have written you on a number of occasions and I don't know if you received any of my letters. I don't know if you're ignoring me, wishing that eventually I'd go away. In either case, I want to thank you for the wonderful times we've had together and to let you know I've found someone else. We plan to marry in June.

I'm sorry if this hurts you, but I haven't heard anything from you in so long, I felt that I had to get on with my life.

I wish you all good things in the future.

Always,
    Madie.

Madie agonized for hours over those few lines and mailed it the next day, hoping that somehow he might receive it.

With Paul's good-bye letter on its way, her thoughts focused on Don, their wedding, and their life together. She still had her doubts, though. Was she doing the right thing by marrying him?

Chapter 15

Madie and Don, and Gia of course, moved forward with wedding plans. By mid-February, things had shaped up nicely. And through it all, Madie wondered if Paul had ever received her last letter. An occasional memory drifted through her mind, a glimpse of them together walking hand in hand along the beach, would cause her to shake herself out of her reverie and get back to the task at hand—her new life.

Just when Madie had convinced herself that she had moved on, her phone rang one day at work.

"Madie here. Can I help you?"

"Madie, luv, it's Paul."

The voice, the words, fell like a stone into her lap.

"My, God, Paul. Where have you been? Are you all right? What's happened? Did you get any of my letters?"

"Oh, Madie, I'm so sorry I haven't written or called. I've been in so much financial trouble and needed to clear some things up, before I could call you."

"But did you get any of my letters?" Madie asked again.

"No, luv, not a one. How many did you send? When did you send them?"

"You've got to be kidding. I wrote you all last year and then finally again last month. How could you not get any of them?"

"I don't know. Maybe someone intercepted them. It's been known to happen, you know."

Madie wasn't sure if she believed him, but continued the conversation. "Well, Paul, I don't know what to say, except that in the last letter I sent you, I told you that I'm getting ready to marry someone."

Silence reigned on the other end of the line.

"Paul, are you there?"

He cleared his throat. "Yes, luv, I'm here. Just a bit stunned, you know. Well, you're not married yet, so no harm done. Not really. We can pick up where we left off."

"Paul, I don't know about that."

"Madie, can you honestly tell me you love him the same way you love me?"

"Paul, I'm too upset to think straight right now." Then she hung up the phone.

Yes, she still loved him. Yes, she still wanted him. Yes, she still wanted a life with him. But damn! She pounded her fist on the desk. Why did he have to call her now? Why couldn't he have called her just six weeks ago before things had gotten so out of hand with Don?

She felt betrayed by her feelings. She felt betrayed by Paul for not keeping in contact with her. The only one who hadn't betrayed her in this whole mix was Don.

Paul didn't call back, and she wanted to cry because she knew she still loved him. Then she began to question why she had agreed to marry Don. Did she truly love him or was he just someone she felt she needed in her life at the time? By now she thought for sure that she'd never hear from Paul again, but he did call back the next week.

She didn't even get the chance to say hello before she heard his voice on the phone. "Don't say a word, just listen. I love you and I'm not going to give you up to anyone. I didn't get your last letter. I didn't get any of your letters. But I still love you. Do you hear me?"

"Paul, I don't know what your intentions are, but I'm engaged to someone else."

"You don't love him. I know you. I know what we had together. We can have it again. Meet me in Miami next month and I'll prove it to you."

"You've got your nerve! I don't hear from you all year, so I got on with my life. Now I'm engaged and you want me to meet you in Miami. How dare you?"

"I dare because I love you. And it's not nerve, it's love. Meet me, Madie."

Madie hesitated. "I'll think about it. That's the best I can do."

"Look, I'm sorry for not calling you, but I had so much stuff happening, and all of it bad. I didn't want to burden you with any of it."

For some reason, Madie felt he was telling the truth. "But why couldn't you have just called? If only you had called. Listen, just call me back next week and I'll let you know."

Despite the fact that she had led Paul to believe she needed to decide, almost immediately Madie began to make arrangements to go to Miami to meet him. She had to see him one more time to satisfy her curiosity, and the unanswered emotions tugging at her, and possibly to say her final good-byes.

As promised, Paul did call her back the following week.

"Hello, Madie. I know I have no reason to hope, but will you meet me in Miami?" he asked.

"Yes, Paul, I'll meet you. But I can't promise anything."

"That's all right. That's fine. I just need to see you again. I'm desperate to hold you again."

"Paul, I have to tell you I don't know what I feel for you anymore."

"That's all right, too. I know you'll find your love for me once again."

Madie didn't know if she wished for that to happen or not. They settled on a date and where to meet and Madie hung up the phone. Then came the problem of Don. It would be nearly another month before she left for Miami. How could she hide anything from him? She knew he'd sense something was off.

Madie tried very hard to hide her thoughts and intentions from Don, but she was right, he sensed something was amiss.

Then one day he asked her point blank, "Madie, are you seeing another man?"

Madie acted surprised, though she had expected this question--eventually. "Really, Don. How could you ask such a thing? Our wedding is just such an important step in my life. I'm just trying to dispel all doubts.

I'm really not seeing anyone. I was just thinking about someone, and I guess it was more obvious than I had thought."

Don took her hands in his. "I'm sorry. I know this is a big step for you. I know you're doing a lot of thinking, and I applaud you for that. I know you're not the type of woman who would do that sort of thing. It's just that there's something different about you. I can't quite put my finger on it."

"I've just been overworked lately."

Don leaned forward and kissed her cheek. "You know I love you. Never doubt that."

Madie had no idea how she managed to get through the next few weeks, but she did, knowing this trip might change the course of her life once again.

Chapter 16

When Madie walked off the plane, she found Paul waiting for her.

"Hello, Madie. So nice to see you again."

He hugged her, but not closely. He kissed her, but chastely on the cheek. He seemed emotionally distant and this left her puzzled.

He helped her with her luggage and they went to the rental car. They hardly spoke on the way to the hotel, though she wanted to scream.

They checked into the hotel and as soon as they got to the room, Paul excused himself, saying he needed to run a quick errand.

"Really, luv, I'll be back in about an hour," he said as he closed the door behind him.

Madie stood there wondering what was going on.

As promised, Paul returned about an hour later. He walked through the door and headed for the shower without a word. When he had finished, he came back into the room, grabbed her and kissed her hard.

Madie gasped, pulled away from him, and slapped him across the face. "What do you think you're doing?"

He responded with a hurt look.

"You've put me through hell for the last year and now you think you can come over here and kiss me like a desperate man gulping for air? You think that's going to make it all right? I need answers, Paul, and I need them now."

He ran his fingers through his hair and sat on the bed. "What do you want to know?"

Madie folded her arms over her chest. "First off, what had happened that you couldn't pick up the phone to call me?"

Paul sat there for a moment looking at her with such pain in his eyes. "Madie, I'm so sorry for all of it, but when I'm finished telling you what I have to say, you'll understand why. Do you remember me telling you about some court dates?"

"Yes, I remember. What of it?"

"They were concerning a debt that I owed the government. They arrested me and I spent nearly three months in jail."

"If I had only known."

He described his experiences in prison and it was as if each word caused another crack in her heart. She realized how much she really did love him and that her marriage to Don would end in disaster.

"Oh, Madie, only thoughts of you kept me going when nothing else would. I felt I had to come back to you. Then I found you had not only started seeing someone else, but agreed to marry him. I didn't know what to think."

Madie felt like a first-class heel. How could she have betrayed Paul and their love?

"Eventually, my wife and her family came up with the

money I owed, and I was released."

He stood up and pulled her close. "I'm so sorry to have caused you so much pain, Madie." Then he started to cry.

"Paul, please, don't blame yourself. I'm the one who gave up on us, not you. Can you ever forgive me?"

"Madie, I can forgive you anything. I only need to know that you still love me. Do you?"

"Oh, Paul, yes. I've never really stopped loving you, but I've managed to come to care for someone else as well."

"Do you really love him or were you just lonely?"

"I really do care for him, but I didn't love him the same way. We have a mutual respect between us. I had put you totally out of my life and moved on. Are you still living with your wife?"

"Yes, but for the time being I have to. She and her family came up with the money for my release from prison." Madie had her answers, but they just generated more questions and more confusion. "Can we continue our talk tomorrow. Right now, I'm so tired I can't think straight. I need some sleep."

"Of course, luv. Tomorrow."

Chapter 17

"Well, good morning. How long have you been up?" Madie asked as she opened her eyes.

"Since dawn. You were talking in your sleep and you were quite restless last night."

"I know. I have so many mixed emotions right now. I guess I rehashed everything we talked about last night in my sleep."

"Have a little breakfast. You'll feel better." Paul pointed to the tray that he had ordered. "Look, bacon, eggs, toast, all good things to get you started on the day." He filled a plate with a sampling of each of the foods and brought it to Madie in bed.

"Thank you. I think I may finally be hungry." Madie took a bit of bacon.

Paul went to the tray and filled a plate for himself. "So, Madie, are you really going to marry Don?"

She stopped chewing.

"If you tell me you don't love me anymore, I'll understand, and get out of your life forever."

Her heart stood still. She put her plate down, walked over, and hugged him. "I'll always love you, but what can I do about it now?"

He held her face in his hands. "It's not too late. Give him the ring back. Call off the wedding. We can still have a life together."

"How can I go back to Boston and hurt Don like that? He was there for me when I needed him."

"The question is: who do you really want to spend the rest of your life with?"

"Paul, do you think we'll ever be together?"

He held her close. "Yes, Madie, I think we will. Someday. No matter what it takes."

"I love you, Paul, not Don. He's just someone to be comfortable with. I needed someone and you weren't there."

"I know that, Madie. I was just waiting for you to figure it out."

Paul pulled her close and kissed her with all the fire and passion within him. Madie felt as though she were living a dream, and never wanted to wake up.

He caressed her. He kissed her. He sent spasms of pleasure coursing through her body. She let him explore every corner of her body, and she in turn explored him.

She kissed his neck, his face, his lips, as if she had never touched them before. They drove each other mad with desire. They became one with every breath in each other's arms.

His kisses moved from her mouth, to her throat, and lower with each gentle touch, until he reached her most sensitive spot. He brought her to screams of pure joy and exhaustion.

He smiled with the knowledge he had sent her further than he ever had before. She watched him slowly touch her trembling body and call her his Bonnie. They fell in love all over again, and when he finally entered her, she grew weak with love as she saw the pure and honest pleasure in his eyes. They reached the stars together and cried out, then sweetly, warmly lay in each other's arms for what seemed like hours.

In that moment, Madie knew she could never love anyone as she loved Paul. She needed to go back to Boston to tell Don it was over.

"Paul, you need to straighten things out in your life. We need to be together. I know now I can't live without you."

"Oh, my sweet Bonnie. I can't live without you either. I will somehow get things worked out and make it possible for us to be together soon. I never want to be without you again."

Chapter 18

The next morning, Paul took Madie to the airport. He kissed her good-bye as she heard her flight called.

"I love you, Madie. I'll call you as soon as I get home."

Suddenly, Madie had a horrible feeling. She had no idea where it came from but she didn't want to leave him. She had an inexplicable fear of never seeing him again. She only held him close. "I love you too. Let's make it happen for us this time."

She boarded the plane and began her flight back to Boston, but something still churned inside her and made her restless. She tried to tell herself that she was just over-reacting. "Cut it out, Madie," she muttered. "You're making a mountain out of a molehill." But still, she couldn't shake it.

She slept most of the flight back and woke up just as the plane made its final descent into Boston. During her drive home, she tried to figure out how to tell Don that she couldn't marry him.

She knew that no matter what she said, she'd hurt his feelings, but she needed to make the blow as soft as possible, and she had to be honest with him.

She had only been home a short time when the phone rang. She immediately recognized the voice at the other end.

"Hello, Madie, did you make it home safely?"

Her heart sank. "Yes, Don. I did. Thank you for calling. I'm home and everything is fine."

"Great. Can I come over to see you?"

"If you don't mind, can we do it tomorrow? I'm a bit tired and right now, I'd just like to go to sleep."

She heard the disappointment in his voice when he said, "Well, all right then. I can wait until tomorrow. You know, I've missed you very much. I love you, Madie."

"Thank you, Don. Goodnight for now. I just need some sleep."

She hung up the phone and felt a terrible tightness in her chest. She did not look forward to breaking her engagement to Don.

The next day, after work, Madie headed for Don's house. Every nerve in her body felt raw and throbbing. She had no idea how he'd react to the news.

When she arrived, she found him waiting outside for her. He walked out to the car to meet her. As soon as she got out of the car, he pulled her close and kissed her with a deep passion.

She pulled away from him. "Don, we need to talk."

"Madie, what's wrong?"

"Can we go inside? I don't want to do this here?"

"Do what?"

She motioned to the house and he led the way.

"Would you like a glass of wine?" he asked.

"Yes, please." Madie felt she needed something to

steady her nerves.

He poured each of them a glass and sat down beside her. "Okay. Now tell me what's wrong. Whatever it is, we can make it right."

She took a long swallow of the wine. A second or two clicked by and Madie felt a strange feeling come over her. "Could I lie down for a moment? I suddenly feel odd."

And that's all she remembered until the next morning.

Chapter 19

Madie woke up to find herself in Don's bed. She felt strange and confused. She blinked and saw Don walking in, carrying a cup of coffee.

"What happened?" she croaked.

"You must have had an allergic reaction to the wine," he suggested.

"That's never happened to me before."

"Always a first time. You passed out and I stayed up taking your pulse and blood pressure to make sure you were okay."

"Wow. I just must be under more stress than I thought. Thank you for taking care of me, but I need to get dressed and go home now."

"Really, Madie, you need to rest. I need to go to the office, but feel free to stay as long as you like."

"I really don't feel well. Maybe I'll stay for a bit."

"Good girl. Take care of yourself." He leaned forward and kissed her on the cheek. "I'll call and check on you later."

She heard the front door close and then the sound of his car leaving the driveway. Madie couldn't believe this had happened to her. She felt so weak. She rested for another hour or two before she dressed and went home.

Again, she had only been home a short while when the phone rang.

"Are you feeling any better?" Don asked.

"Still a little weak, but better."

"I'll come by to check on you after I've finished here at the office. If you need anything at the store I'd be happy to stop and get it for you."

"Thank you, no. I think I have plenty of everything here at the house."

Madie slept most of the afternoon and woke up to find Don sitting next to her.

"Sorry if I've startled you. Are you hungry? I made some soup for you."

Madie gave him a weak smile and sat up. "Yeah, I think I'm a little hungry."

"Good, stay right there."

Don went to the kitchen and brought back a tray with soup and juice. Madie ate most of it and felt a bit better after eating, but her head was still swimming a little.

"I don't know, Madie. I'm worried about you. If you're not better in a day or two, I'm going to order some tests for you."

"Thank you for your concern, but I'm sure I'll be better by tomorrow."

"Do you need anything before I leave?"

"I'm fine, really. The children will be home soon."

He kissed her check. "Call me if you need me."

Madie felt relieved when she heard him leave the house. She just didn't like him standing over her as though she were a child.

The next day, she felt much better and went into the office, and Paul called shortly after she arrived.

"Is everything all right?" he wanted to know. "I've tried to call for the past two days but got no answer. I've been worried about you."

"No, I'm fine. I was just a bit under the weather, but I'm better now."

"I'm so relieved to hear your voice. I love you so very much."

"I love you too, Paul. I can't wait to be with you again."

"Have you told Don yet?"

"No, but I've been a bit ill. I'll tell him soon. I'm feeling much better now and need to get this done."

"I'll call you next week about the same time, so make sure you're there."

"I promise. I will be."

Don called later in the day and asked how she felt.

"Better thanks, and thank you for taking care of me."

"Madie, would you stop by my house after work?"

"Sure. I can do that." Madie thought that might be the perfect time to drop her bomb.

She called home to let her children know that she'd be late.

"That's okay, Mom. I need to get some photography paper for a class, but I'll leave a note for the other kids."

"Fine. I'll see you later. You do have Don's number in case you need me, don't you?"

"Yeah, Mom. Relax. We'll be fine."

Just as Madie made ready to leave the office, Don walked in.

"What a surprise, Don. I was just on my way to your place."

"Well, I decided we needed to have dinner together. It's been too long."

Madie held her breath. "I really need to talk to you in private, but I guess it can wait."

They shared a pleasant dinner and then Madie followed Don back to his house.

"Would you like something to drink?" he asked as they entered the door.

"Yes, thank you. A martini would be nice."

He fixed their drinks and then sat beside her. Madie sipped her drink as he told her about his day and some of the patients he had seen. He leaned back on the sofa and relaxed.

Don moved closer to her and whispered in her ear. "Madie, I need you so much. I never want to lose you."

His words made her feel uneasy and scared at the same time.

"Don, I have something to tell you."

Very deliberately, he placed his drink on the coffee table. "I know, Madie. You were with Paul."

A sharp pain shot through her.

"I hired a private detective to follow you when you went to Miami."

A sudden fear of him grew inside her. She tried to stand but her legs felt like rubber and she couldn't move.

"I'm not going to give you up, Madie. You know, you should have never gone to see Paul."

Madie tried to speak but the words just wouldn't come. She didn't know what was wrong. She felt so strange.

"I assure you. You'll never see Paul again. And do you know why? Because you won't want to."

Madie nodded.

He got up and fixed her another drink. For some reason, Madie felt a peace settle over her, but didn't question why.

"You're my life, Madie. I want you for my wife and I will have you for my wife. So get used to it."

He led her into his bedroom and removed her clothes. She knew she wanted to stop him but couldn't. He started making love to her and Madie felt as though she had fallen into the rabbit hole. He took her hard and Madie felt the tears coursing down her cheeks. She had no control of anything happening to her; as if someone else had taken over her mind and body. Hour after hour he came into her, invaded her.

She couldn't see what he was doing, but felt an excruciating pain. Between her tears she asked, "What are you doing to me?"

With a growl in his voice, and anger in his eyes he answered, "I'm making you mine, and I'm making sure you stay mine."

She hoped that this was all a bad dream, and that when she woke up, she'd find herself in her own bed, wrapped up in Paul's arms. Somehow she managed to go to sleep. When she woke up the next morning, she found herself in Don's bed.

She blinked against the sunlight coming in through the window, and winced an unfamiliar pain at her core. At that moment, Don walked into the room carrying a cup of coffee.

"Good morning, sleepy head. How are you this morning?"

Madie pulled the sheet up to her neck and backed up against the headboard.

Don handed her the coffee. "What's wrong, Madie? Have a bad dream or something?"

With her voice shaking in anger and fear, she asked, "Don, did you rape me last night?"

He threw back his head and laughed. "You've got to be kidding. I'd never do that to anyone, much less you. I love you. Whatever put that idea in your head?"

Her body and her feelings told her one thing, but her intellect told her to believe him. They must have just made love last night and then she had fallen off to sleep and had a nightmare. That was it. That had to be it.

Don sat by her on the bed and spoke in a tender voice. "Madie, we made love last night. Mad, passionate love like never before. In fact, you were the one who started it. I couldn't believe it, but I loved it."

Madie finally took the coffee he offered. The warmth made her feel better. Don started kissing her neck then slowly moved to her breast. She didn't want him to stop. He felt so good. He moved his fingers inside her, and though she felt sore, she wanted him to continue.

On some level, Madie knew something was wrong, but she didn't know what it was, and she couldn't stop it.

"You don't ever want to see Paul again, do you, Madie?"

As though she had no control, she answered automatically, "No, Don, never again."

For the rest of the day, Don made love to her. She

wanted him, but she didn't. She wanted to stop him, but she couldn't. She felt so confused.

That night she asked, "Don, what's happening to me?"

"Oh, Madie, I'm just making sure that you remain mine forever."

"Don, why would you think anything else? Of course I'm yours." The words spilled from her lips, but other words had formed in her mind.

Before he left her for the night, he put her hands into restraints.

"What are you doing to me?" she asked frantically.

"Madie, my dear, I have to punish you for what you did to me."

Fear surged through her but she said, "Yes, I know. I deserve to be punished."

Eventually, Don removed her restraints and allowed her to move about the house.

She cooked dinner one evening and Don said, "You're such a good wife, Madie."

Madie gave him a confused look. "Don, when did I become your wife?"

"Madie, don't you remember? About a week ago."

"Where were we married?"

"Right here in the house."

He had all the answers, and Madie grew more confused than ever.

She couldn't remember any of the ceremony or anything else.

"I want to thank you, Don, for giving me the honor of becoming your wife. I hope to always make you happy."

"I know you'll make me happy, sweetheart."

"Don, where are my children?"

"They're with their father and doing fine."

"Why aren't they here with me?"

"Well, you know, we're starting a new life and all that. I asked your ex if he'd keep the kids for a while. He said it was fine with him."

Madie didn't recall any of this, but believed him. She started feeling as if she were watching this drama from out of herself.

She didn't know what Don was doing, but she knew it wasn't good. On some level, she knew she had to get out of here, but she didn't know how. For some reason her world revolved around Don, her new husband.

Then suddenly one day, Don said, "Madie, you know, I think it's time you went back to work."

"I don't know, Don. I'm not sure I'm ready."

"You will be by tomorrow," he said. "Get yourself ready."

Madie agreed. "Sure. That sounds good, but please help me understand what has been happening to me."

He smiled. "We've just had an extended honeymoon and now it's time for us to get back to work."

Madie again accepted his explanation and thanked him for his help. That night, they made love most of the night before he finally allowed Madie to go to sleep.

The next day, when she returned to work, Gia squealed as she walked in the door.

"There she is! The new bride!" Gia hugged her close. "So are you happy now? How was the honeymoon? How's Don as a husband? Is he all you thought he'd be?"

"Wow, how long have I been gone?"

"Silly. You've been gone for two months. What a honeymoon. Tell me all about it."

Madie gave her a weak smile. "It was wonderful." She didn't know what else to say. She didn't remember much.

"I have to admit I was a little worried when Don called and said that you two had decided to elope on the spur of the moment, but I knew Don would make you happy," Gia said.

"Yes, he's made me very happy." Madie looked around at the familiar surroundings. "Well, now, Gia, let's get to work. Where are we?"

Gia filled her in on things and Madie plunged right in. She closed a deal that Gia had put together, but found it difficult to concentrate at times. Madie felt a great relief at the end of the day when she could close up her desk. It had been difficult for her.

Don picked her up after work and took her home. He seemed so loving and he cooked dinner that night, and afterward, Madie said, "I'd really like to lie down for a while. I'm not feeling very well."

"Sure, Madie, go make yourself comfortable. I'll bring you a drink." For the life of her, she couldn't figure out why she suddenly began to feel so bad.

Just as she started to doze, Don came into the living room with a drink. "Here you go. Some white wine. That should help whatever ails you."

As she reclined on the couch, she suddenly began to feel very strange. "Don, what was in that drink you gave me?"

"Nothing. Why would you ask such a question?"

"I don't know. I was feeling better there, for a while

and now, I'm feeling strange again."

"You're probably just tired. It was your first day back at the office."

She didn't argue with him. Instead, she sat beside him. He pulled her close.

"Madie, I love you. Never forget that."

He made her feel safe, but she continued to question many things in her mind.

The next day at work, Madie's phone rang. She immediately recognized Paul's voice.

"Madie, are you okay? I've called time and again over the past two months."

"Paul, so nice to hear from you. I'm fine. I hope you're doing well. What can I do for you?"

"What do you mean, 'What can I do for you?' Have you gone mad? What's happened to you?"

"To tell you the truth, Paul, I'm not really sure, but somewhere in the last two months I married Don. Now that I'm married, I'd appreciate it if you wouldn't call me again."

"Madie, I have to tell you, you don't sound like yourself. I've got to see you to make sure you're all right."

"Paul, I'm not a child. I'm fine, and you don't need to worry about me." Then she hung up the phone.

Madie immediately felt as if she had just done something she didn't really want to do. None of this made any sense to her and she began to question her sanity.

She looked up when Gia walked into her office.

"Are you okay, Madie?"

"That was Paul on the phone and I hung up on him."

"What? That man has been calling here almost every

day for the past two months. He's worried sick and crazy about you."

"I didn't know, but it doesn't make any difference. I'm married to Don now."

"That is so not like you. I think you need to see a doctor."

"Look, I'm married to a doctor, and if I need care, Don will take care of me."

Gia just turned and left the office, slamming the door behind her.

Madie felt like she needed to go home so she called Don to come pick her up.

Don arrived within the hour and she told him what Gia had said.

Don replied, "Don't worry about her. She's just a busybody. You're fine, and if you ever need a doctor, I can take care of you."

"That's just what I told her. And, there's something else."

He nodded to encourage her.

"Paul called, but I hung up on him."

A broad smile filled his face. "I'm so proud of you for telling me about this."

"Don, I have to ask you something."

"Go ahead. What is it?"

"Is something wrong with me?"

He laughed. "Why would you ask such a thing?"

"Don, it really bothers me that I can't remember much from the last two months. I mean, I can't even remember our wedding."

"You're fine. Now stop worrying over nothing."

Madie smiled at him. "I'm glad you came to pick me up. Do you think I really need to work?"

"No, you don't need to. I just thought you'd like to."

Madie smiled shyly. "No, I'd really prefer to stay home to make sure I please you. That's all that matters to me."

"That's fine with me, Madie. Why don't you ask Gia if she'd like to buy you out?"

Later that evening, Madie did just that.

"Madie, are you sure? I can't believe you'd sell it after all the work you've put into it."

"It's just not that important to me anymore. I just want to get rid of it."

"Well, in that case, I'll give it some thought."

"Fair enough, Gia. See you tomorrow."

Don beamed at her. "You've done the right thing, Madie."

She felt happy that she had pleased Don so much, yet, she questioned if she had indeed done the right thing.

As she cooked dinner, Don brought her a drink, and started kissing her. "Why don't you put dinner on hold? We can do something that's a lot more fun."

"Mmmmmm," she responded and followed him up to the bedroom.

Don lowered her onto the bed and began to explore her body. He ran his hands over every inch. He pinched, and teased, and pressured. Madie lay in a muddle of sensations and enjoyed his attentions.

"Madie, do you like this?" he asked in a husky voice.

"Oh, yes, Don. Don't stop. I love it."

"Good, girl. I'm going to take you someplace tonight,

that I know you've never been to." As he said that, he rose from the bed and walked across the room to the closet. He emerged with several lengths of silk.

Madie gave him a puzzled look. "What have you got there?"

Don lifted his finger to his lips. "Shh. Just enjoy."

He took one of the lengths of silk rope and bound her right wrist to the headboard.

"What are you…?"

"Shh," he repeated. Then he bound her other wrist.

A terrible fear began to creep through her. Then he took two more lengths of silk and bound her ankles to the bed.

"Don, this isn't funny," she said timidly.

"I don't intend for it to be funny." Then he blindfolded and gagged her.

Madie nearly panicked when the blackness closed in on her, but she had no freedom of movement, no way to protest. Next, she felt a coldness inside her, and an intense heat on the outside of her body. She had no idea what was happening to her. Then something entered her from behind. The scream of pain came from her throat, but could not emerge.

She heard his sadistic laugh pierce the blackness and she wanted to run, but could barely breathe. She prayed for God to somehow help her make sense of what was happening.

She felt a slap across her face, but in defiance fought back the tears. Then the realization hit her. Her prayers had been answered. In her sudden epiphany, she realized that Don had been drugging her and abusing her. She felt sick to her stomach and wanted to retch.

"What's wrong, bitch? Don't you like this anymore?" He slapped her across the face again.

He pushed something long and cold into her to cause more pain. She grew more humiliated and degraded by the minute, but at the same time, she began to find strength. She knew she had to play his game if she were going to survive this nightmare.

She pretended to enjoy his abuse, and he grew less aggressive in response. He even uncovered her mouth to give her a drink.

"I knew you'd love it," he said.

Madie drank the whole glass of water.

"So do you still love Paul? Do you still want to be with him?" Don growled.

"Of course not. You're the only man for me. How could you ask such a question? You're the only man I could ever love."

"Right answer, Madie."

Despite all she had just endured, Madie started to relax, and thought it strange. Then she understood. Don had drugged her again. Don went back to work, using and abusing her as never before. She felt as though he were trying to pull her insides out. For whatever reason, he seemed to take great pleasure in causing her great pain. He didn't stop until he finally relieved himself.

She felt him leave the bed, then heard him leave the room. She breathed a sigh of relief despite the fact that she was still bound to the bed. Madie fell asleep, relieved that her ordeal was over. But when she woke, Don knew it. He had returned to the bed during her slumber.

"Finally awake, sleepy head? Good. Time to play again."

This time he seemed more determined to cause more intense pain.

"Oh, Madie, I love you. I'll never let you leave me," he whispered as he slid yet another implement inside her.

Fear turned to terror and Madie felt herself shake uncontrollably.

"Mmm. Look at the effect I have on you." He uncovered her mouth. "Now tell me who you love."

"I love you. You. Nobody else."

Don went back to work and Madie blacked out.

The next morning, when Madie awoke, Don had already removed the restraints and washed her body.

"Good morning. How are you?"

"Fine. I guess. But tired." She gave him a sideways glance. She felt as if she were married to Dr. Jeckle and Mr. Hyde.

"So call Gia and tell her you're not feeling well today. You'll go back to work when you're feeling better."

He handed her the phone and Madie did as he asked.

The same scenes played out day after day. Madie doubted her sanity, her rational abilities, her emotions, and her reality. She didn't know which end was up. She only knew she feared this man who claimed to be her husband and that she wanted to escape him.

Night after night, Don took her most cruelly; raping her, drugging her, raping her again until she passed out.

03030303

Paul, unable to contain his worry about Madie, called her office.

"Gia, it's Paul. Is Madie there?"

"Paul, good to hear from you. No, Madie's not here. You know, I'm worried about her. I haven't heard from her in a couple of weeks. She doesn't call and she doesn't answer her phone."

Then, in a determined voice he said, "I'm coming to Boston."

Madie awoke in a fog. Strange sounds and smells surrounded her. She barely croaked out a sound. "Help me please."

A nurse in scrubs walked into the room. "Well, nice to see you've joined us."

"What do you mean?" Madie asked.

"You've been out of it for a couple of days."

"What's wrong with me?" Madie asked.

"You're going to be just fine."

"Why am I here? How did I get here?"

The nurse never had a chance to answer. Madie had fallen fast asleep and slept through until the next morning. When she looked around, she remembered that she was in the hospital. When she tried to get up, a sharp pain jolted through her.

A nurse came in to check on her. "Good morning."

"Hi. Can you tell me why I'm here? What's wrong with me?"

"I'll call the doctor. I'm sure he'll be able to answer all your questions. You just rest until he gets here."

Thousands of thoughts ran through her brain. She tried to formulate all her questions in preparation for the doctor's visit. When he arrived, his pleasant smile reassured her.

"Hello, there. I'm Dr. Fannin. Do you know your name?"

She gave him a half smile. "Of course I know my name. I'm Madie Robertson."

"Ding. Ding. Ding. Right answer. So how are you feeling?"

"Sore. Very sore. What's wrong with me? Why am I here? I tried to get up but couldn't for the pain. Tell me what's wrong."

The doctor pulled a chair close to the bed. "Madie, I don't want you to get upset because it's all over now. But you came to the emergency room alone, with no identification, and showing signs of shock." He studied her closely.

"When was that?" Madie asked.

"Three days ago."

Stunned, Madie stared at the doctor with her mouth open.

"We've all been very concerned about your mental state, because you kept having nightmares and waking up screaming."

"What hospital am I in?"

"Boston Memorial. You're in very good hands."

Madie gulped.

"Do you know a Dr. Don Shaver?"

"Sure, I've heard his name. I don't know the man personally. Is he your doctor?"

"No!" she screamed.

"It's okay, Madie. You don't have to have him for your doctor if you don't want him."

"Do you want me to call your family?"

Madie shook her head. "No, thank you. I'll call them. But would you please explain what's wrong with me?"

He gave a deep sigh. "Ms. Roberston, I'm not sure how to tell you this, but when you came into the hospital, you were suffering from severe abdominal pain. When the ER doctor examined you, he was surprised you were alive, because it looked as if somebody had tried to, I'm not sure what somebody tried to do to you, but they almost succeeded."

"What are you talking about?"

"Madie, you were in bad shape when you arrived here. We had to remove your uterus, repair damage to your vagina, urethra, and rectum. In short, you've been rebuilt inside and out."

Madie couldn't believe what she had just heard.

"Madie, do you know who did this to you?"

Through the tears, Madie nodded her head and said, "Dr. Don Shaver."

"No, Madie, we left the subject of Dr. Shaver minutes ago. Who did this to you?"

With a steely gaze, she stared into Dr. Fannin's eyes. "Dr. Don Shaver did this to me. You need to call the police."

"I have to tell you, we also found a variety of drugs in your system."

Madie nodded. "Every night he'd drug me and rape me. I had no control of anything. I didn't know what was happening to me."

"That explains a lot. The drugs we found in your system were mind-altering drugs. Madie, I suggest you call someone, maybe someone in the family, a close friend. I think a little TLC could do you a lot of good right now."

When the doctor left, Madie reached for the phone to call Gia.

Gia arrived within the hour. "Madie! There you are!" she screeched.

Her antics brought a smile to Madie's face. "Shh, this is a hospital."

"Well, maybe it's about time somebody did a little cheering up, up and down these morbid halls. How are you? What happened to you?"

Gia sat in the chair beside the bed and reached to embrace her friend. The tears immediately flowed as Madie began to remember little bits of pieces of the past months.

When Madie had told her friend her story, she gave her a job to do. "Please, Gia, call the police. Don did this to me."

"That explains so much. Do you remember me telling you weeks ago that I thought something was wrong with you?"

Madie nodded.

Gia did as Madie asked and when the police came to the hospital, Madie gave them a full statement of all that she remembered.

Chapter 20

Madie stayed in the hospital for another ten days and tried to recall everything that had happened to her. The police came by to see her twice to tell her that Don had disappeared and they couldn't find him.

The policeman said, "We've also contacted his sister, but she hasn't seen him since their mother's funeral. We contacted his ex-wife, but she said she had no clue where he might be."

"He couldn't' have disappeared without a trace."

"No, ma'am. But we're not about to give up."

Detective Knowles, the lead detective on the case said, "We want to see this man behind bars and I'll do everything within my power to put him there."

"Thank you, Detective. Is it possible to get a restraining order just in case Don ever shows up again?"

"Sure, you could get one, but I don't believe this scum will ever show his face around here again. You call me if you need anything," he said as he left.

Madie tried to get some rest, but every time she closed her eyes, she saw Don's face, or heard his laugh. Try as she might, she could not escape him.

On her last day in the hospital, Gia stopped by the

hospital to visit her friend. "So have you talked to Paul yet?"

"Paul? How could Paul know I'm here?" Madie asked.

"Ah, hmm, he's been calling, you know."

"You didn't tell him anything did you?"

"No, no, only that you were in the hospital. He's frantic you know."

Madie turned her head away. "I can't let him see me like this. Besides, I'm no good to him now. I'm no good to any man."

"Oh, Madie, you know that's not true. So, you can't have any more children. Truly, did you want any more? You already have a wonderful handful. And the doctors say you're going to heal up just fine. You have your whole life ahead of you. You love Paul and he loves you. Why deny yourself the happiness you can find in each other?"

"Oh, Gia, I don't think I could ever face him after this."

"Nonsense. It's reality. It's what happened to you, but it's behind you now. Put it behind you and look to the future."

Madie choked back her tears. "Do you think Paul can do that?"

"I can if you can." A deep, masculine voice came from the doorway.

"Paul? Is that really you?"

"In the flesh. May I come in?"

"Yes."

Slowly, Paul walked toward her and reached for her hand.

Gia stood. "Well, I guess you two would like to be

alone. Pick you up tomorrow at ten to take you home, lady." She leaned over for a quick hug and waved on her way out the door.

Paul sat on the side of the bed and hugged her close. "It's so good to see you."

"I'm glad to see you too. You'll never know how glad I am to see you."

"I think I have some idea. You're just as beautiful as I remembered."

"I can't begin to talk about the horrible things that man did to me."

"You don't need to, Madie. Maybe someday it won't be so hard. When you're ready, I'll be there." He pulled her close. "I'm so thankful you are alive and doing better."

Then he began to tell Madie his side of the story.

"Madie I came to Boston to find you, but Gia didn't know where you were. No one knew. Gia only said that you had married Don and were still on your honeymoon, but I had this horrible feeling that something was wrong. She gave me Don's address and so I went out to his house.

"I knocked, but no one answered the door. I heard voices from inside, so I knew someone was there. I rang the bell. I pounded on the door, but anyone and everyone inside ignored me. So I found an open window and let myself in. I followed the angry voice and found myself outside your bedroom door."

Madie turned away in utter embarrassment, thinking of what horrible thing he must have seen.

"I found you bound to the bed with a blank look on your face. God only knows what you had suffered, but I knew I had to get you out of there. Then Don came out of the bathroom and saw me there. I reached for something heavy, I don't even know what it was, but I hit him over the head and knocked him out.

"I found your pulse and called 9-1-1. When I knew help was on the way, I took Don out to my rental car."

"And what did you do to him?"

"Don't ask me, Madie. Just know that you have nothing to fear from him ever again."

"Paul, please, you can't let the story drop there."

"I called someone from my old drug running days. He told me where to bring Don and I turned him over to this dude then left. A little while later I got a phone call that said that Don had suffered before he died and that his body will never be found. My only regret is that I didn't get to you before he did."

He began to cry. "Can you ever forgive me?"

"Forgive you for saving my life?"

"I'd do it again if I had to."

"I know you would and I love you for it." She hugged him back.

Epilog

Madie recovered from her terrible ordeal. Paul divorced his wife and moved to the States. Paul and Madie married and her children grew to love Paul very much. He never mentioned the fact that they could never have children, but Madie has come to a point in her life where nothing is more important than the love she and Paul share, and the future they are making together. And what a beautiful future that is!

To order additional copies of
Enduring Love

Name _____

Address _____

_____

_____

$12.95 x _____ copies = _____

Sales Tax   _____
(Texas residents add 8.25% sales tax)

Please add $3.50 postage and handling   _____

Total amount due: _____

Please send check or money order for books to:

Special Delivery Books
WordWright Business Park
46561 State Highway 118
Alpine, TX 79830

For a complete catalog of books,
Visit our site at
http://www.SpecialDelivery.com

Printed in the United States
69076LVS00001B/132